:te
/.
ep

0'

Leaning down, Spence kissed her forehead.

The light touch of his lips set off a chain reaction of shivers that had more to do with her internal engine than with the snow and cold. Her inner machinery had definitely come back to life. She exhaled on a soft moan.

"What else?" he murmured.

Resisting him wasn't going to be easy. "Nothing much."

"It's okay. You can tell me."

But maybe she'd better not. Though his tone was gentle and cajoling, she knew he was digging, probing, interrogating. If he discovered the gaps in her memory, what would he do? He said he was a federal agent, but that didn't mean he was innocent.

She turned the tables with a question of her own. "What do you do for the FBI?"

Frozen Memories
CASSIE MILES

First Published in Great Britain 2017
By Mills & Boon, an imprint of HarperCollins*Publishers*
1 London Bridge Street, London, SE1 9GF

Large Print edition 2017

© 2017 Kay Bergstrom

ISBN: 978-0-263-07242-6

Printed and bound in Great Britain
by CPI Antony Rowe, Chippenham, Wiltshire

Cassie Miles, a *USA TODAY* bestselling author, lives in Colorado. After raising two daughters and cooking tons of macaroni and cheese for her family, Cassie is trying to be more adventurous in her culinary efforts. She's discovered that almost anything tastes better with wine. When she's not plotting Mills & Boon Intrigue books, Cassie likes to hang out at the Denver Botanical Gardens near her high-rise home.

A salute to the geniuses who work at
NORAD and still manage to run the
Santa Tracker every Christmas.
And, as always, to Rick.

Chapter One.

Jagged branches clawed the arms of her sweatshirt and tangled with her bare hands as she fought her way to the edge of a clearing in the mountain forest. Falling snow blanketed the open space. Spears of afternoon light cut through the snow and clouds, but she still couldn't see all the way across, to the wall of pines on the opposite side. She shivered violently. If she tromped straight through the clearing, she'd leave tracks. They'd find her.

Who were they, those men with guns? What did they want from her? She peeked over her shoulder but didn't see them following. Her ears prickled, but she didn't hear them coming after her.

They'd left her on the floor in the back of the van. She hadn't moved, hadn't opened her eyes. They must have thought she was unconscious. One of them had nudged her with his steel-toed boot, but she hadn't given any sign of wakefulness. They'd talked about whether or not they should take her into the cabin with them. And they had decided not. They hadn't wanted to carry her. If she froze in the van, they didn't care.

Glad that they were so stupid, she'd waited until they'd gone inside. Then she ran. Without a parka. Without mittens. Without boots. Wearing only sneakers and a hooded sweatshirt over a flimsy pair of hospital scrubs, she'd staggered into the storm. The cold should have awakened her, but she'd felt lethargic. Her legs were heavy; her feet weighed her down like cement boots. She lurched through the trees, uncoordinated, unable to keep her balance.

As she'd gone farther, her physical abilities had improved. But that didn't mean she was out of the woods—literally out of the woods. *Making an unfunny joke, I messed up the punch line.* Still, she chuckled. When she stretched her mouth, her lips cracked. *I always wanted to die laughing.*

My God, what was wrong with her? She ought to be terrified. Instead, she felt oddly giddy and confused.

The gusting wind threw icy flakes into her teeth. Her clothes were cold and wet. Her shoes soaked through. She'd seen photos of people who were frostbitten, with their fingers and toes turning black and falling off. But she'd also heard that dying of hypothermia was supposed to be peaceful, like drifting into a gentle sleep.

Sleep would be good, maybe just for a minute. Her eyelids closed. She imagined a boat pulled by snow geese with a glittering snow god at the helm. All she needed to do was climb aboard. Looking down, she smoothed the white feathers of her gown. Sleep was so very good. *Or not!* Delusions were a symptom of hypothermia. Her mind was going. She needed to find warmth as soon as possible. Leaving a track across the clearing was a small price.

She charged forward with the storm beating at her head and shoulders. The accumulated snow was almost up to her knees. When had it started? When would it stop? With the sun blocked out by the snow clouds, she could only guess that it was afternoon.

Reaching the forest on the other side was a relief. She staggered up a hill. Her lungs throbbed. Her thigh muscles ached. She shivered madly.

Then she saw lights.

Nothing had ever been more beautiful. As she moved closer, she realized she was approaching a snow-packed road, a large building and a two-story cabin with lights in the windows. *Left, right, left, right,* she lurched toward the glow, the warmth, the light that would save her. Closer and closer, she tried to call for help but her throat was as frozen as the rest of her.

The larger building beside the house was a church with a snow-covered cross above the entrance. These had to be kind, decent people who wouldn't turn her away. *They had to be.*

She climbed the two stairs to the wrap-around porch. With the last of her strength, she knocked.

The door was opened by a barrel-chested man with a neat, white beard. He wore a plaid flannel shirt and red suspenders. At the far end of the room, a fire danced on the hearth.

"My dear girl," the old man said. "Come in and get warm."

She stumbled across the threshold into a charming, pine-paneled cabin with dozens of photos on every wall and cute knickknacks on every flat surface. The main features—apart from the fireplace—were a long dining room table with enough room to seat fourteen and an upright piano. As the old man closed the door, heat shimmered around her and wakened her senses. Her skin tingled. She'd made it. She was alive, painfully alive.

The sounds of classical music rolled down the staircase, and a woman's voice called from the second floor. "Clarence, is someone here?"

"It's a young woman, Trudy. The poor thing is half froze."

"She's out in this weather? Good heavens, I'll come down and help you take care of her."

"Okeydoke."

Lacking the strength to remain standing un-assisted, she clutched the back of a chair. Her vision blurred. The prickling of her fingers worsened. Her skin was on fire.

"Take it easy." The old man braced his arm around her. "You're going to be all right."

She looked up at him. His cheeks were rosy, and his eyes were a bright blue that matched a stripe in his plaid shirt. She moved her mouth, wanting to thank him, but no words came out. When she licked her lips, she tasted blood.

"I'm Clarence," he said. "Pastor C. W. Lowell."

She noticed his short, military haircut. "Air force?"

"You are correct. I was a chaplain for twenty-three years." He looked into her eyes. "Now you know all about me. Let's hear about you. What's your name?"

Her mind was blank. Her name, what the hell was her name? She could have made something up but didn't want to lie. And so, she spoke the truth. "I don't…remember."

"Not surprised," said a small woman in a long nightgown and bathrobe as she shuffled down the staircase. "I'm Trudy, and you're probably in shock."

I'm in shock. That must be it. She squeezed her eyes shut and clenched her jaw against the flaring pain. Everything burned—her arms, her thighs, her hands and feet, her nose, even her earlobes. She would have passed out, but gentle hands guided her into a tiled bathroom. Trudy shouted directions to her husband while she seated her on the closed toilet. Together, she and Trudy peeled off her wet clothing and shoes.

"Dry off with the towel," Trudy instructed while she grabbed fresh clothing from the pastor, who stuck only his hand into the bathroom. "These jammies ought to fit. They belong to my granddaughter, and she's your size. How tall are you?"

"Five feet nine inches."

"I used to be tall." Trudy glanced into the mirror above the sink, gave herself a smile and adjusted her long silver braid. "Lately, I've been shrinking."

"Still beautiful," she said, and she meant it.

"Later, we'll get you into a bath. For now, we need to warm you up slowly and get your blood circulating. You're not frostbitten but close. Hurts, doesn't it? You're very brave."

She appreciated the compliment. Though running away from those thugs didn't seem particularly courageous, she'd survived what was clearly a bad situation. What if the bad guys came this way? "Danger," she mumbled, "dangerous men…they're after me."

"You're safe now. Clarence doesn't look like a tiger, but he's a very good protector."

She fastened the last button on the warm, dry pajamas and stumbled to her feet so she wouldn't fall asleep on the toilet. Though her skin still stung like fire, she felt stronger as she hobbled into the front room. After sinking onto the sofa, she pulled up the wool socks on her poor, frozen feet and tucked a fuzzy yellow blanket around her shoulders.

Pastor Clarence placed a mug of fragrant lemon tea on the coffee table. "Don't drink too fast," he warned.

"But you need to rehydrate," Trudy said.

She nodded and took a sip. "I want…to thank you."

"You're doing much better." Trudy handed her a tube of lip balm. "Are you well enough to recall your name?"

Carefully, she applied the salve to her cracked, chapped lips. Her mind was blank. "Maybe… in a minute."

Trudy sat in the overstuffed chair nearest to the sofa and tucked her robe snugly around her. "You said there was danger."

"Yes."

"Let's ease into your memories gradually," Trudy said. "What's the last thing you remember?"

"A van…there was a van…men with guns."

Trudy shot a nervous glance toward her husband, but her voice stayed calm. "What color was the van?"

She took another sip of tea. The liquid soothed her throat. "I think it was black...or dark blue."

"I want you to concentrate," Trudy said. "Tell me about the men. How many of them? Did they say each other's names?"

"Four of them. One had an accent... Southern, I think."

The pastor scowled. He went to a window at the front of the house and peered into the storm, on the lookout for danger.

"Where was the van parked?" Trudy asked.

"At a cabin...a log cabin."

"And what did this cabin look like?"

"I think the door was painted green."

"One story or two?"

She cleared her throat. The words came more easily if she whispered. "Don't know... I couldn't see it very well through the trees and the snow. Those men...they might come after me. I didn't cover my tracks very well. I'm sorry."

"You did the right thing, getting out of the storm, and I appreciate the warning." Clarence opened the door to the front closet and reached up to a high shelf. "If we've got wild-eyed criminals running around in my forest, I sure as heck want to be ready for them. What else can you tell me?"

"Their weapons were HK417 assault rifles."

"That's mighty specific, little lady. How come you know so much about guns?"

She shrugged.

"You might be in the military." He took a hunting rifle down from the shelf and set it by the door. Then he removed a long wooden box from the closet and carried it to the table.

A sign flashed in her mind. "Peterson Air Force Base."

"That's not too far from here. Is that where you're stationed?"

"I don't know. I don't think so."

Another image replaced the first. She was staring into the maw of a tunnel large enough to drive a couple of semitrucks through. This huge half circle abutted the mountain, Cheyenne Mountain. It was the entrance to the underground NORAD complex, and she wasn't supposed to talk about it—not even with nice people like Trudy and the pastor.

She'd said too much already, should never have given her trust so freely. What did she really know about Pastor Clarence and his wife? Nothing! The pastor unloaded a SIG Sauer and two Colt revolvers from his wooden box. Plus there was the rifle by the front door. These two definitely weren't helpless woodland creatures.

"Honestly, Clarence." Trudy rolled her eyes. "If you're going to play with your guns, put down some towels so you don't scratch my table."

He put the revolvers away in the box and

tucked the SIG into his waistband beside his suspenders. "I'm going upstairs. The windows up there make better vantage points."

"Before you go," Trudy said, "would you please call 911? I'd like to get the sheriff up here. And an ambulance."

"Not for me," she said.

"I'm afraid it's necessary, dear."

She didn't want to go to the hospital. Turning herself in would violate her mission. *Her mission? What mission?* "I'm already feeling a lot better."

"Except you can't remember your name." Trudy leaned forward to pour. "More tea?"

"Yes, please." She studied the older woman. Trudy's movements were disjointed, her right arm seemed stiff, and her hands were twisted in a knot. Under her flannel gown and robe, she was very thin, possibly sickly. "If I can borrow a coat, I'll be on my way."

"Don't be silly." Trudy's voice was sharp

edged. "In this weather, you won't make it a mile. I didn't haul myself out of bed and help you get warm only to have you go running outside to freeze again."

"You're right." She sank back against the sofa. "I'm sorry…for waking you up."

"I wasn't sleeping, just lying down. It's too early for bed."

"She has rheumatism and a nerve disorder," Clarence explained as he picked up his cell phone. "There's only so much we can do to alleviate the pain. The one thing that relaxes her is music."

"I used to be a music teacher," Trudy said with a wistful smile. "And I'm still the choir director at our church."

When she'd first entered the cabin, she'd heard a symphony from upstairs. "You didn't have to turn off your CDs because of me. I adore classical music."

"You're sweet to say so," Trudy said.

She sat up straighter on the sofa, roused by a vivid memory. "I play the violin."

"Do you?" Trudy lightly applauded. "I'd love to hear you play."

If it would keep them from sending her to the hospital, she could play all the Mozart concertos with Beethoven thrown in on the side. She'd do whatever was necessary to evade the danger that encroached on all sides. From the thugs in the van to the vicious storm to her unnamed fear of being hospitalized, everything appeared to be against her. She felt as doomed as a skier racing downhill, trying to escape a churning, roaring avalanche. Her chance of survival was slim.

Chapter Two

Through the ragged curtain of falling snow, FBI Special Agent Spence Malone spotted headlights approaching. "About time," he muttered.

Spence wasn't running this operation, but his directions had summoned two vans—one for the local SWAT team and another from the FBI—to this isolated mountain cabin with a dark blue van parked in front. It had been twenty-seven minutes since he called for immediate emergency backup.

His tension was epic. When it came to making sharp, street-smart decisions, he trusted the instincts he'd learned at an early age in foster care. But this assignment was different. Not only was he dealing with a global situation, but his partner was the woman he loved.

Spence feared that he'd made the wrong decision by not going after her when he found the van. He could easily have followed her tracks into the forest. But he'd wanted to make sure these four thugs were apprehended and secured. Backup was required.

He bolted from his rented SUV and charged toward the vans. The SWAT commander and an agent in an FBI jacket joined him on the road. A wall of pine trees separated them from the cabin.

After introductions, Spence filled them in. "My partner is missing, and I think these men grabbed her."

"Her?" Ramirez, the agent, yanked off his FBI watch cap and combed his fingers through his thick black hair.

"Agent Angelica Thorne is NSA, not FBI.

We're partners for the duration of this assignment." And the assignment was top secret. They didn't need details about Angelica. "I followed her tracking signal to the van and checked inside, where I found evidence."

"Evidence?" Ramirez questioned.

"Her prints and hairs," Spence said dismissively. "Trust me, she was in that van."

"But not anymore," Ramirez said.

"As far as I can tell, she's in the wind. But she left these four goons behind. I've been observing them with a heat sensor. They're all in the kitchen."

The SWAT commander gave a quick nod. "Armed and dangerous?"

"Yes," Spence said. "I've got questions for them and would appreciate if you keep them alive."

"Consider it done," the commander said. "I'll deploy two snipers in the trees, just in case. And we'll storm the house from the front and side."

"Go for it," Spence said. "I'm sitting this one out."

He and Ramirez returned to his SUV, where he picked up his rifle, infrared goggles and a backpack. He needed to hurry. Dusk had fallen. Soon, it would be dark.

"Should I come with you?" Ramirez asked.

"Not necessary." If Spence couldn't find Angelica, he might as well throw himself off the nearest cliff. He wouldn't be able to live with the guilt if he lost her. "I need you here to take those four into custody."

"No problem. We've got a cage at headquarters that's just the right size."

Ramirez chewed on his lower lip. Spence guessed the other agent was fighting to suppress his excitement. There probably wasn't much action at the FBI offices outside Colorado Springs. Spence held up his cell phone. "Call me when they're in custody."

Ramirez exchanged numbers with him. "Tell me about the NSA agent. How did she get grabbed?"

"This is the first time Agent Thorne has been in the field."

"Inexperienced," Ramirez said with a disgusted shake of his head. "Am I right? The chick is a typical rookie."

"Don't say *chick*." Spence retrieved his phone. "And there's nothing typical about her."

"Sorry, man." Ramirez raised both hands, placating. "I'll call when we've got these guys."

Spence took off at a jog, heading into the forest in the direction he had already tracked. It wasn't her fault that she was missing. It was his. He shouldn't have left her alone, not even for a minute. If his brain had been working, he would have refused to be her partner in the first place. This assignment wasn't the type of thing she was accustomed to handling.

Angelica worked in the Cyber Security branch of NSA. She'd been there for three years and had a reputation as an outstanding hacker. Though she usually stayed behind her desk, she was chosen for this assignment because her dad was a retired general in the air force who lived in the area. People around here knew her family, and the gates of the North American Aerospace Defense Command, or NORAD, complex were more likely to open for somebody familiar and friendly. As soon as they'd arrived, she'd proved useful in cutting through military red tape. He wasn't sure if that was due to her high-ranking contacts or her dynamite body.

He saw her footprints in the snow. Branches had been broken on the pine trees. She'd come this way. He dug into his pocket for his GPS device. The blip from her implanted tracker was loud and clear. She was close, less than a mile away. He dared to hope that she'd be all right as he moved quickly through the trees.

She'd charmed him six months ago, on the first day they'd met at Quantico, where she'd come to do a consultation. If he'd been a movie producer looking for a woman to play the part of a secret agent, Angelica would have been number one on his list. She was five feet nine inches tall with long, slender legs and classic curves. Her black hair fell straight and sleek to her shoulders. And she was stylish in high-heeled boots, tailored clothes and expert makeup that showed off her mysterious green eyes. One thing was for damn sure, Angelica didn't look at all like a computer geek—which was exactly what she was, an NSA expert called in to advise on an FBI hack.

To say that he and Angelica got along well together would be an understatement. From their first kiss, he'd known that she was special. They'd started dating after that first case was closed, which shouldn't have been a dating-in-the-workplace problem because he never expected to work with her again.

Behind his back, he heard the sounds of the SWAT team assault on the cabin. His shoulders tensed as he listened for gunfire. First, there had been three loud explosions from flash bangs. Then there were loud shouts. He counted gunshots. One. Two. A spray from an automatic, two more, then there was silence. The whole thing had taken less than five minutes, a good sign. Quick operations were usually successful.

He hoped that his and Angelica's mission would also be swift and effective. They were investigating an attempted hack at the supposedly impregnable NORAD complex. With Angelica's technical expertise and his experience in undercover ops, their collaboration should have gone smoothly, except that she'd been abducted within twelve hours of their arrival.

At a clearing in the forest, he paused. Obvious tracks went straight across the middle. The fact that she hadn't taken time to disguise her route told him that she must be desperate. He charged across the snow and up the hill on the opposite side.

Spencer saw the lights of a cabin beside a church, an obvious safe haven against the storm. The wind had erased most of her tracks, but he still saw indentations as he rushed toward the two-story cabin. The lights were less than ten yards away. He could smell the smoke that rose from the chimney.

The gentle strains of a violin wafted through the air as he pulled off his glove and rapped on the door. There was no answer. He hammered more loudly and shouted, "Open up. FBI."

The door opened, just a crack, and a voice commanded, "Step back."

When Spence saw the barrel of a rifle, he decided to cooperate. An elderly, bearded man came out onto the wide, covered porch and pulled the door closed. There was a Santa Claus thing going on with the white beard and the red suspenders, but this old guy wasn't jolly and smiling. He aimed his Remington at Spence's chest. *Bad Santa.*

"I'll need some ID," the man growled.

Spence reached inside his parka pocket and took out his badge. "I'm looking for someone."

"What for?"

"She might be in danger."

"I'm going to let you inside. But if you make one false move, you'll be sorry."

As soon as the door opened, Spence saw her. With perfect posture, she perched on a wooden chair, wearing flannel jammies and playing a violin.

He called out, "Angelica."

Abruptly, she lowered the bow and stared at him.

An elderly lady, who seemed to be the mate of the man who opened the door, chuckled. "Angelica is a perfect name for you, dear. You play like an angel."

"A snow angel," her husband said.

Unable to keep his distance, Spence strode across the room toward her. He needed to gather her in his arms, to stroke her hair and whisper reassurances that he would never leave her unprotected again.

"Stay back." She stood and faced him. "How do you know my name?"

ANGELICA, MY NAME is Angelica. She thrust and parried with her violin bow, fighting to keep the guy in the huge parka away from her. *Angelica!* The word echoed inside her skull, and she liked the sound. It felt right. She remembered a rowboat with that name written in fanciful letters across the stern. *And so, Angelica, what are you going to do now?*

"He claims to be with the FBI," Clarence said.

"We'll see about that." Her first priority was

to deal with Parka Guy. "Give your rifle and backpack to Pastor Clarence."

He spread his hands. "I'm not going to hurt you."

She touched the tip of her bow to the center of his chest. The slender, fiberglass stick looked ridiculously delicate and flimsy against his girth and strength. His shoulders were as wide as the Frankenstein monster. He could snap that bow in half and use the horsehair strings as a garrote if he felt like it. For that matter, he could snap her in half, too. If she had any sense at all, she'd be shaking in her socks.

More forcefully, she said, "The rifle. Do it."

In a few swift moves, he unfastened the rifle. He also removed the backpack, which he held toward her. When she didn't take it, he growled and dropped the pack on the floor next to his gloves.

He unzipped the front of his parka and flipped back the fur-lined hood. His complexion was ruddy from being out in the snow, and he had a tiny scar on his chin that she somehow knew he'd gotten in a barroom brawl. Everything else about him was perfection. Square jaw, wide mouth, high cheekbones and the most intense, ice-blue eyes she'd ever seen. His gaze was mesmerizing and predatory like a wolf.

"Now," he said as he thumped his very solid chest. "You recognize me now, right?"

Though there was something familiar about his towering height, the pattern of stubble on his chin and the blond streaks in his hair, she couldn't say for sure that she knew him. And she really wanted to. It'd be a shame to beat this handsome man to death with her violin bow.

"On your knees," she snapped. "Hands behind your head."

"Oh, my," Trudy said with a gasp. "Sounds like you've done this before."

Had she? Where were these commands coming from? How did she know what to do when threatened? Classes… She remembered the exercises; she'd taken training. Every agent in her division was required to learn the basics of law enforcement and firearms. "Quantico," she whispered.

"That's right," he said. "You trained at the FBI facilities."

The FBI? She was an agent? It hardly seemed possible that a real federal agent would attempt to subdue an attacker with a violin bow. "I don't think I'm in the FBI."

"You're in the NSA, in the Cyber Security division."

Sure, why not? She turned away from Gorgeous Parka Guy, flipped the violin onto her shoulder and played the opening notes of "Blackbird" to show there were no hard feelings. Perhaps a silly, delusional thing to do, but it seemed like a positive gesture.

Angelica asked Pastor Clarence, "Would you please reach inside his jacket and disarm him?"

"Wait," Parka Guy said. "I can save us a lot of time if I take off my own weapons."

"Fine." Angelica perched on the edge of her hard-back chair and continued to play the classic Beatles song. She segued to "Yesterday."

Concern about Gorgeous lingered in the back of her mind, but she wasn't scared of him. The opposite, in fact. She felt safe, ridiculously safe considering that she'd just escaped from four thugs and she was some kind of agent who had special training. She really ought to worry, especially since he was carrying two Glocks, an eight-inch serrated hunting knife and a small-caliber pistol in an ankle holster strapped above his heavy-duty boots.

Stripped of his weapons and his parka, he approached her, stood and waited for her to finish her violin solo. Gently, he took the instrument and the bow from her hands and laid them on the long, wooden dining table. He came back to her, leaned down and gazed directly into her eyes. "Say my name."

Her breath caught in her throat. The whirlwind of confusion buffeting inside her head went still, and she was suspended, floating in midair. She felt neither cold nor hot, neither right nor wrong, neither safe nor terrified. She was simply there.

"Spencer," she said. "Spence Malone."

And then she was in his arms. The cold from outdoors still clung to his Irish fisherman's sweater, but the internal heat from his body raised the temperature. She snuggled against him, inhaling the natural scent of lamb's wool and warm man.

He whispered in her ear, "You couldn't forget me."

Apparently, she'd guessed correctly.

Chapter Three

Now she knew his name was Spence Malone, but Angelica had no idea what that meant to her. He was incredibly good-looking, just exactly her type. She glided her hand across his rock-hard chest and down his arm. Even through his thick sweater, she felt the ridges of his biceps. Were they lovers?

He tilted her chin so she was gazing up at him. His blue eyes flicked from left to right, reading her expression. "Seems like you've forgotten a few things," he said.

"A few." She shrugged.

"What do you recall?"

"There were four men, big guys, dumb as dirt." His penetrating gaze was like a truth-seeking missile, and she wasn't sure how much she should reveal. She turned toward Trudy and said, "Remember? I told you about them. One had a Texas accent. They were armed with HK417 assault rifles. They took me to a cabin."

"And she mentioned a van," Trudy said helpfully, "a dark blue or black van."

Leaning down, Spence kissed her forehead. The light touch of his lips set off a chain reaction of shivers that had more to do with her internal engine than with the snow and cold. Her inner machinery had definitely come back to life. She exhaled a soft moan.

"What else?" he murmured.

Resisting him wasn't going to be easy. "Nothing much."

"It's okay. You can tell me."

But maybe she'd better not. Though his tone was gentle and cajoling, she knew he was digging, probing, interrogating. If he discovered the gaps in her memory, what would he do? He said he was a federal agent, but that didn't mean he was innocent.

She turned the tables with a question of her own. "What do you do for the FBI?"

"Mostly administrative stuff," he said in a silky voice. "Do you remember where we are?"

"Near Peterson Air Force Base." Luckily, the pastor had provided her with that much info.

"Do you know why we're here?"

"For one thing, my parents live near here." Before she could think twice, she said their names. "Peter and Lana Thorne."

"General Thorne?" Pastor Clarence straightened his posture, almost as though he was snapping to attention. "You're their daughter?"

"One of their daughters," she corrected.

Her memories came fast and furious as a mental family portrait formed. There were two girls and two boys. Angelica was second or third

oldest depending on who was doing the counting. She and her sister, Selena, were identical
twins, and they always argued about who was
born first. The youngest—a boy who chose
the marine corps over the air force, much to
his father's chagrin—had moved out last year.
Though Dad was mostly retired, her parents
kept their six-bedroom house in the hills above
Manitou Springs.

She was looking forward to visiting them and
having them meet Spence, which meant he must
be important to her. Since it wasn't her habit to
introduce casual lovers to the parents, Spencer Malone must have a different significance.
Maybe she worked with him. He was a born
leader, similar to her high-ranking father. Both
were tough, competitive and feisty.

She gave him a grin. "You and Dad are going
to love each other."

The gleam from his cool blue eyes dimmed.
"You introduced me to your father yesterday."

"Indeed." *Couldn't be. That's not something I'd forget.* She treasured every moment with her mom and dad. Family was everything to her.

"We were at their house for dinner. You don't remember?"

"Give me a minute. It'll come back."

He sat her on the hard-back chair. His touch became less sensual and more clinical as he massaged her scalp. "Does your head feel sore? Is there a possibility of concussion?"

"I was afraid of this," Trudy said as she clenched her fingers into a knot. "It's amnesia, isn't it?"

"Maybe," Spence said. "She needs a CT scan. And she ought to be examined by a doctor."

"We put in a 911 call," Trudy said. "It felt like an hour ago."

"I'll call again," Clarence said. "They warned me about slow response time on account of the weather. And there was a pileup accident on I-25. When I told the dispatcher she wasn't bleeding and didn't appear to have broken bones, he suggested I drive her myself if it was possible."

"I'll take care of it," Spence said.

"Wait!" Angelica waved both hands to interrupt the plans that were being made for her. She was wide-awake, sitting right here, and she didn't like having other people take control of her life. "I don't need a hospital. I didn't hit my head."

Spence hunkered down in front of her. He captured her fluttering hands and held them. "Would you remember if you had?"

"Did you find any bumps on my head?" she demanded. "No, you did not. And my skull doesn't feel concussed. There are plenty of other places on my body that are painful, but not my head."

"Where does it hurt?" he asked.

"My lips are chapped and were bleeding." She

yanked her hands from his grasp. "My feet are stiff and sore. My throat is scratchy."

"She has bruises," Trudy said. "I noticed them when she was changing clothes."

Shrinking back in the chair, Angelica wrapped her arms protectively around her midsection. She knew very well that she had injuries. Both her knees were scraped. A massive contusion spread from her rib cage to her lower pelvis on her right side. Though she couldn't see her back, she felt an occasional throb of pain.

The physical damage might have come from a hard fall or a car wreck. She might have been beaten but didn't remember, didn't want to remember. She'd been doing her best to ignore these aches and get back to the business at hand—whatever that was.

She glared at Spence. "No way do I have a concussion."

"There are other ways to lose your memory."

He placed his hand on her knee, reestablishing contact. "You could have been drugged."

She glanced down. Her eyelids closed. For an instant, she caught a glimpse of what had happened. A brief sliver of memory revealed itself, and she saw things as they had occurred instead of as they were now.

Her wrists were fastened to the arms of a chair with duct tape. She wasn't uncomfortable but firmly secured, immobile. Behind her back, disembodied voices talked about dosage. They mentioned a drug.

She repeated their words, "A derivative mixture of benzodiazepine and propranolol."

When she looked up, she saw Spence nod. "Those are drugs that could be used to induce memory loss."

"I knew that." Oddly enough, that was her first outright lie. She knew zip about drugs and memory loss, but she wanted desperately to speak with some kind of authority.

"If you were drugged," Spence said, "we need to take you to the hospital for tests. Be reasonable, Angelica. I want you to be checked out. I feel responsible."

"Please don't."

"Don't what?"

"Feel responsible."

She bolted to her feet. Even though she couldn't exactly identify her career at the moment, she was dead certain that she was well respected in her field. She'd always been an achiever, proud when her slacker sister teased her for being "daddy's little darling." Ever since Angelica hit her first home run in T-ball, she'd been a winner. Valedictorian and senior prom queen in high school, magna cum laude from college, and she'd received dozens of grants in computer cryptography, science and hacking.

The past was becoming clear to her. She worked at the Cyber Security division of NSA and focused on cryptography and hacking. Her long-term memory was reassembling itself. The short-term still eluded her.

In any case, she didn't want to be tucked away in a hospital. Though she didn't know why, being here—in the field—was an opportunity for her. Going into the hospital meant admitting defeat. She needed to convince Spence that she was okay, and they should get back to work. "I'm fine."

"Do you remember dinner?" he asked.

"Of course, I do."

"Prove it."

Dinner at the home of General and Mrs. Thorne with one outside guest followed a certain ritual. Angelica, along with her brothers and sister, had attended hundreds of Lana's simple but elegant dinners. This one wouldn't be much different.

"The centerpiece on the table was made of pinecones painted orange and blue..." It was football season, and her father was a season ticket holder. "In a salute to the Denver Broncos."

"What did we talk about?"

She knew this one: the primary topic for every true Bronco fan. "We discussed the quarterback. Elway was mentioned."

Spence nodded, and she brightened. *I'm going to get away with this.* She continued, "Mom served Cornish game hens and cheesy potatoes. The pie was pecan."

She could tell by his expression that she'd nailed the menu of her mom's favorite dishes. "Is that accurate?"

He gave another terse nod. "Do you remember why we're here?"

She took a leap of logic. He was FBI; she was NSA. He had come looking for her. "We're on assignment together."

"I still want you checked out," he muttered. Then he looked toward Pastor Clarence. "Can you give me a ride to my car?"

"Sure, but I need to dig out the driveway to the garage. And that might take half an hour or forty-five minutes."

"I'll hike," Spence said as he started loading his weapons back into their holsters. After he slipped into his parka, he picked up the extra-large backpack and dropped it at her feet. "I brought your clothes, boots and a jacket. While I'm finding the car, you can get dressed."

"I'm not going to the hospital," she said firmly. "I'll call my dad. He can pick me up."

"Not a chance." Spence forced his words through a tight-lipped grin. "I want General Thorne to like me. That's sure as hell not going to happen if I tell him how I slacked off on the job and let his daughter get kidnapped. And then, even worse, I have to call him for help."

Though Angelica didn't want to turn to Daddy for help, she considered having Spence rescue her to be equally frustrating. She hefted the pack by one strap and slung it over her shoulder causing a pain that crawled up and down her spine. She held her breath and willed the hurt to stop. She didn't have time to be injured. She refused to be taken out of the game.

Spence said she was kidnapped. *Kidnapped?* That must be why those thugs had her in the van and why he'd been searching for her. "Did they demand a ransom?"

"No."

Well, of course not. Kidnappers wouldn't ask the FBI for money. "What about my father? Did they contact him?"

"This isn't about money," Spence said. "At least, it's not about the piddling amount that a kidnapper could demand."

She didn't understand. If her kidnappers hadn't been after money, why did they take her? "Is it because—"

He stepped up close, interrupting before she said too much. He gave a quick glance over his shoulder at Clarence and spoke to her softly. "We'll talk about this later."

"But I—"

"Later." He took the backpack from her grasp, asked directions from Trudy for someplace private and carried her pack up the staircase and into a guest bedroom. Pillows were stacked at the head of a queen-size bed, and the brightly patterned duvet was neatly made. With the door partially closed so the pastor and his wife couldn't hear, Spence whispered, "I'm guessing that they kidnapped you because of the computer codes you were working on before we left. That's the bad news. The good news is that you must have hit a nerve. You're on the right track."

"Would computer codes be worth more than a ransom?"

"Hell, yeah." He raked his fingers through his sun-streaked hair. "The weapon codes stored at NORAD can be used to activate, launch, deploy and shut down various missile and satellite systems, mostly for ICBMs. Foreign governments would pay a small fortune for that information."

"I got it."

"Do you remember the kidnappers or what you told them?"

"I'm drawing a blank." What if she'd given up the codes? She might have already betrayed their mission. This investigation might have a real unhappy ending. "I'm sorry."

"Once we get back to the hotel, I have a technique that'll help you remember." He took her hand and gave it a squeeze. "Get changed. I'm going to pick up the car."

When he left her alone in the bedroom, Angelica placed the backpack on a cedar chest at the foot of the four-poster bed, which was one of the few surfaces free from knickknacks or photos. She unzipped the main compartment. The soft beige turtleneck, the jeans and the lightweight, superwarm Patagonia jacket were familiar. As she changed into the clothes, she remembered when she'd bought them, remembered trying them on, washing them and taking them out of the dryer. Her memory seemed back to normal, except for recent events.

It was as if a neuroprogrammer had reached into her skull and erased chunks of her brain. Last night and yesterday were totally blank. Until Spence had explained the investigation at NORAD, she didn't know why she was here. What kind of computer hacking did she do? Who taught her? And then, there was Spence. He was the most fascinating puzzle of all. She remembered him but didn't know if they were tangled in a hot-and-heavy relationship or if they were just friends.

When she raised her arms to slip the turtleneck over her head, her torso twisted and she felt a stab of pain from the big, nasty bruise on her side and hip. Unwilling to admit how truly lousy she felt, Angelica forced herself to stand erect. Wearing her own clothing felt good. Even better, she found a makeup kit and toiletries in the backpack.

Confronting the mirror that hung above the dresser was horrific. From her snarled black hair to her chapped cheeks to her hazel-green eyes, which were road-mapped with red squiggles, she was a mess. How could Spence even look at her without gagging? If she ever hoped to find out what kind of relationship she had with him, damage control was necessary.

After she combed her hair, put on lotion and dabbed at the worst parts of her face with makeup, she looked around the guest bedroom. On the top of the dresser was an army of clay figurines that were obviously sculpted in kindergarten classes. And there were tons of framed photos of kids in costumes, playing games, skating and skiing.

Trudy was the opposite of Angelica's mom, who kept tidy scrapbooks and limited her displays to formal pictures, such as wedding photos, graduation pictures and framed diplomas. Angelica figured she was more like Trudy, favoring snapshots of kids with dirty faces and stolen moments caught on film. She liked to think that pictures were a good way to capture memories, her memories.

Eyes closed, she attempted to focus. She visualized the headquarters where she worked, an attractive space filled with bold artwork, curving corridors, horizontal windows and computer screens with cascading streams of numbers. She imagined her desk in a smallish, orange-and-white office with a window, an ergonomic chair and a white desk that extended the length of one wall. Her gaze zoomed in on a framed photo of her and Spence, laughing and embracing. In another intimate picture, they were holding hands and walking at the edge of a frothy ruffle of surf.

The sound of a ringtone from downstairs pulled her out of her reverie. Spence's ringtone, it played the opening notes to *Camelot.* He'd changed it to that theme after they saw a revival of the musical at the Arena Theater.

Vivid images of what happened after they went back to the hotel after curtain call rushed through her. She tasted the fizz of champagne, smelled the scent of fresh roses, felt his huge hands encircling her waist as she opened her mouth for his kiss. The definitive answer to one of her questions became clear. Their relationship was anything but casual. Deep and intense, they were lovers.

Chapter Four

Spence zipped up his parka and took his cell phone outside onto the snow-covered porch that stretched across the front of the cabin. The caller ID displayed: "SA RAMI." It had to be Special Agent Ramirez calling to let Spence know that the SWAT takedown was successful. But the first words Ramirez said were, "I'm sorry."

"Why?"

"One of the suspects got away."

He launched into an explanation of what had happened at the nearby cabin, but Spence stopped him. "That's enough."

"You need to understand that—"

"You and a trained team of SWAT officers failed to apprehend four mindless goons in a sneak attack." In spite of the cold, Spence was steaming. "Spare me the details."

"It wasn't my fault," Ramirez complained.

Spence hadn't forgotten that SA Ramirez was quick to sneer at Angelica's rookie status. "Is SWAT in pursuit?"

"They are, but this guy got out of his cuffs, grabbed a weapon and—"

"He's armed?"

"Oh, yeah, he was slick. He took off like a jackrabbit. They aren't going to catch him."

And why aren't you chasing him? Spence had little respect for feds like Ramirez who left the real work of law enforcement to the cops while they stood around posing in their black suits and their FBI windbreakers. Part of Spence's investigation at NORAD would include checking out Ramirez's office, and he wouldn't be surprised to find a mole. Even a half-assed spy wouldn't have much problem outsmarting the likes of Ramirez. His boss, Supervisory Special Agent Raquel Sheeran, was another story. She was as sharp as a stiletto.

Spence ordered, "Arrange for the three in custody to be delivered to the FBI offices."

"I already have."

The escaped thug complicated the situation. Spence couldn't leave Angelica and the elderly couple unprotected while he hiked back to pick up his vehicle. But he wanted to get Angelica checked out by a doctor as soon as possible. Being in two places at one time wasn't an option.

Though he hated relying on Ramirez, he needed help. He leaned against the porch banister and peered toward the church next door. Though the storm was pretty much over, a blanket of snow lay heavy on the unplowed road and the parking lot. Night was starting to fall, but it wasn't totally dark. The glow of starlight filtered through the clouds.

"Ramirez, I want you to drive here. Bring one other man." Spence gave directional driving instructions and used Pastor Clarence's address for Ramirez's GPS. "Do you understand?"

"Got it."

"I'll be waiting."

Pastor Clarence came onto the porch. In spite of his age and potbelly, he moved with the stealth of a hunter. "I can help you find that van at the cabin," he said. "Angelica mentioned a green door. I know exactly where it is."

The old man wore a red knit cap, again making Spence think of Santa. But the pastor's red gloves were clutched around his rifle instead of a bag of toys. The parka that was belted around his ample midsection was black.

"I'm getting picked up," Spence said. "Besides, you need to be here when the ambulance arrives."

"The sheriff can figure it out. He's a real crackerjack."

"Yeah? Well, he's not winning any prizes as a first responder." Spence had to consider the possibility that sweet old Clarence hadn't, in fact, contacted the emergency dispatcher. Santa might be lying. "How long ago did you make that call?"

"A while." He tugged on his beard. "Something's fishy. What was your phone call about?"

"There's a dangerous armed man on the loose. I'll get Angelica to the hospital. An officer from SWAT will be left behind to protect you and your wife."

"I can take care of my family." Clarence puffed out his chest. "I don't want some SWAT punk hanging around."

"You need protection." Spence was fairly sure the old man was hiding something but didn't have time to dig for the truth. "The punk stays, and that's an order."

"Hah!" The pastor threw back his head. "I've been retired for fourteen years. I don't obey orders unless they come from my sovereign."

"Who's that?"

Clarence pointed skyward. "My Lord in Heaven."

Spence gazed across the snowy crossroads toward the dark, impenetrable forest. A shaft of moonlight illuminated the simple cross above the church's entryway. Clarence was a man of God, but that didn't mean he was without sin. "What does your Lord say about lying?"

"You know the Commandments."

"Do you?"

The pastor fidgeted and sputtered, and Spence could see the truth struggling to get out. If he stood here quietly and waited, Clarence would confess whatever he'd been holding back.

The pearly white landscape spread before him, so ethereal and beautiful that he almost ran inside and grabbed Angelica to show her.

Better that he didn't; she might not be enthu-siastic about the wonders of snow after being nearly frostbitten to death. The only marks in the unbroken snow were his tracks and Angel-ica's. Hers were almost erased by the drifting wind.

At the edge of the forest, he saw movement. It could be deer or elk or his own imagination, but he didn't think so. He took his night vision goggles from a parka pocket and held them to his eyes.

He saw a man, staggering from the forest. He disappeared behind the church. A moment passed while Spence waited anxiously for the man to reappear.

Beside him, the pastor cleared his throat. "There's something I ought to tell you, Spence."

"Not now."

"It's important."

A light shone through an arched window at

the far end of the church. The man—the fugitive—had found sanctuary. Or so he thought.

Spence grabbed the pastor's arm and spun him around. "I saw the fugitive, the man who escaped custody. He's in the church. When the agent and the SWAT officer get here, send them in that direction."

"What about me? I could be your backup."

"Stay here. Protect Trudy and Angelica."

Spence pivoted and leaped from the porch. His boots hit the snow, and he started running toward the church. The new-fallen snow slipped over the top of his boots and soaked his jeans. He ducked behind a clump of aspen and inhaled a deep, frigid breath. At this elevation, oxygen was scarce.

Between the trees where he was hiding and the front entryway to the church, there wasn't much cover. If he stood upright and ran, he'd be an obvious target. But there wasn't time to dash around to the road and come up from the front.

He kept his repeating rifle slung across his back, choosing instead to arm himself with a handgun for easier mobility. His new Glock 17 fit neatly into his hand. Through the specially woven, nonslip fabric of his glove, he hardly felt the cold of the Glock's handgrip. Keeping his head down and shoulders bent, he tried to make himself small as he rushed toward the front entryway under the cross.

Light continued to shine through the window in the rear part of the building. Was the fugitive standing there, looking out and taking aim? This guy wouldn't be caught napping; he'd managed to get out of his handcuffs and evade a team of trained officers. Ramirez had called him slick, and Spence agreed.

The preferred method for taking a suspect was a straight-on assault, using the element of surprise, yelling to disorient the suspect and being ready to shoot first. But Spence wasn't looking for a lethal shoot-out. This fugitive was low on the totem pole. His greatest value was the information he could give. Somehow, Spence needed to sneak into the church and take the fugitive into custody.

At the entryway, he leaned against the polished oak door with a small diamond-shaped stained glass window at eye level. The church building was a rectangle, with stained glass windows on either side. Spence wasn't sure what he'd find inside. Ruefully, he realized, it would have been useful to have the pastor with him to give him the layout.

The door on the right had a keyed knob. Spence gave it a twist and found it locked. No problem, he'd been picking locks since he was a trouble-making teenager. This was the first time he'd done it at a church.

After turning the knob, he opened the door a crack, slid inside and closed it. The entryway was in darkness. No windows here. In the nave, where the congregation sat, the stained glass windows on either side allowed moonlight to fall across several rows of wooden pews. He edged his way down the wall, expecting—at any moment—to hear the blast of a repeating rifle.

No sound came. And Spence didn't see the fugitive. At the front of the church, there was light from a door at the far right side of the sanctuary. In the entryway, Spence found himself at the foot of a narrow, wooden staircase that hugged the wall. He climbed to a choir loft. Three rows of pews and an upright organ were faintly visible. Quiet as a cat, he crept down to the carved railing, where he squatted and waited.

It was a pretty little church, simple and clean, with a high peaked ceiling and open beams. The carpet in the sanctuary was slate blue and the altar was carved from dark wood. From outside, a fierce wind buffeted the stained glass windows, causing the old structure to creak and moan. *Not a bad thing*, he figured. Those noises had masked the sound of his entry, allowing him to scoot across the back and up the stairs without the fugitive noticing.

A certain amount of skill was required to move with stealth and purpose. But Spence also believed in luck. Being in a church, he wondered if he should shoot off a prayer. He wasn't a religious man, didn't make it to church every week, nor did he quote from the Bible or other sacred texts. But he was spiritual. He believed in a higher power. When he was growing up, two men were instrumental in helping him pull his life together. One was a pastor, the other a priest. Spence had never done a whole lot of praying, but he felt like those church people had done a lot of praying to make sure he stayed on the right path.

A telephone rang. Spence heard the mumbled reply. Was the voice coming all the way from that back room? If so, the acoustics in here were incredible.

The light from the back room went out. The phone call must have tipped off the fugitive. But how? Who made that call? Behind the shadows of the pulpit and a standing candleholder, Spence saw a man dodge across the sanctuary, slam into the side of the altar and then duck behind it.

From his superior vantage point in the choir loft, Spence peered over the banister rail. The element of surprise was gone, but he could still give this guy a chance to make it easy on himself.

"FBI," Spence called out. "I don't want to hurt you. Just put down your weapon and step out from behind the altar."

"What if I don't?"

"I need to take you into custody."

The fugitive laughed. "That doesn't work for me."

Spence heard a voice from behind his back. "Sorry, Spencer. Doesn't work for me, either."

He looked over his shoulder and saw Pastor Clarence, aka Bad Santa, aiming his rifle at a lethal point between his shoulder blades. The old man was working with the bad guys. "This explains a lot."

"What?" Clarence asked.

"You never called 911."

"Nope."

"And I'm guessing that the van hadn't ended up in this area by coincidence. Tell me, Pastor, do you own the cabin with the green door?"

"I do, and three others in this area." He gestured with the rifle. "I want you to stand up real slow and careful."

Seriously? Had Bad Santa forgotten how well armed Spence was? Did this old guy think he could take down a federal agent in his prime?

"Let me remind you," Clarence said, "I've got the drop on you, and it'd be easier to swab up the blood from your dead body than to sand bullet holes out of the pews."

"Were you even a chaplain?"

"I'm retired, but I served."

Something must have happened to turn the old man into a traitor. In other circumstances, Spence might have been willing to delve and probe and put together motivations and answers. But he wasn't in a forgiving mood. This investigation needed to be over so he could return to Virginia with Angelica and repair her memory.

Lowering his rifle and sliding his handgun onto the pew, Spence turned sideways in the choir loft so he'd present a narrow silhouette to the man hiding behind the altar. "Tell me, Clarence, if I hadn't come along, what would you have done to Angelica?"

"What do you mean?"

"She's a loose end. It doesn't seem smart to leave her running free. Would you have shot her?"

Clarence huffed as he adjusted the barrel on

his rifle. "You've got this wrong. Just give me a minute and let me explain."

A disembodied voice rose from the altar. "It's not as bad as you think."

How do you know what I think? Spence had never been known for his calm, patient attitude, and he sure as hell didn't need advice from some dumber-than-dirt thug. It was time to take control of this situation.

Disarming Clarence would be a piece of cake; the old guy wasn't exactly in peak condition. The tricky part would be to avoid getting shot by the armed thug. Spence coiled his long legs beneath him. With one well-placed leap, he went into the aisle between the pews. With a pivot, he launched himself off the organ and smashed into the pastor's broad chest.

Clarence went down with a thud. Flat on his back, he didn't bother struggling. As Spence fastened his wrists with a zip tie, Clarence said,

"There should have been an easier way to do this."

"Explain."

"First, an introduction," Clarence said. "The dark and scary character who escaped the SWAT team is my nephew, Trevor MacArthur. Help us out, Trev. Turn on the sanctuary lights."

The shadowy figure that had been lurking behind the altar went to the edge of the sanctuary and flipped a couple of switches. Lights blazed in the nave.

A young man with curly brown hair and a beard strolled to the front of the sanctuary. "There's one more thing you ought to know, Spence."

"What's that?"

"I'm FBI, working undercover."

Chapter Five

Trust no one. Her father had always advised her to be suspicious and, as always, Dad was right. Angelica had been fool enough to accept the pastor and Trudy as the kindly, elderly couple they appeared to be. *So wrong!*

Frozen in place, she stood in front of the dresser in the upstairs bedroom of the cabin, where every wall was hung with photos and every flat surface held knickknacks. Her gaze stuck on a five-by-seven photograph of a young man in a football uniform. His face and his dark, floppy hair appeared in many other photos scattered around the room.

At first glance, he'd looked familiar, and she wondered if they'd gone to the same school. She'd grown up in this area, and he might be somebody she'd met before or had known. Slowly, she'd circled the room, prowling, taking time to study each photo as the man aged from a skinny kid in baggy shorts to full adulthood. His grin was mischievous, with a twist on the left side. A tiny scar bisected his left eyebrow.

Like a lightbulb snapping to life, her inability to remember vanished. The darkness cleared. She knew him.

This young man was one of the thugs in the van—a kidnapper, a traitor or something worse.

Trudy called out from downstairs. "How are you doing, Angelica? Can I help?"

She moved to the top of the staircase. Her throat was still raw and her voice hoarse. "Changing clothes. I'll be down in a minute."

"Would you like more lemon tea?"

"No, thank you," she said politely.

Her thoughts were far less civil. Dear, sweet Trudy might decide to poison her with lemon-scented bleach. Though it seemed impossible that the kindly choir director was involved with thugs and traitors, the dozens of photos were proof. Trudy knew this man, knew him well.

Unfortunately, there was no chance that Angelica was mistaken in her identification. The memory was crystal clear. His face—with the lopsided grin—had peered down at her several times when she was curled up on the floor in the back of the van. He'd rubbed her upper arm as though he wanted to make her warm, but he'd been the one who insisted to the others that they leave her outside, alone in the van, to possibly freeze.

She needed to tell Spence, and he'd have to arrest these two lovely people who had saved her life. Though Angelica had been trained as an agent, she wouldn't be cool about taking Clarence and Trudy into custody.

Fully dressed and wearing her warm boots, she descended the staircase to find Trudy nestled into a corner of the sofa. Though Angelica had said no, two mugs of tea and a small plate of fragrant banana bread rested on the coffee table.

"Where's Spence?" Angelica asked.

"He and Clarence went running off to chase a bad guy."

Angelica gasped. The bad guy was very likely the man pictured in Trudy's bedroom. And Spence was probably counting on Clarence the Traitor for backup. "I need to find them, right away."

"You shouldn't go out," Trudy said. "We've barely got you warmed up. The last thing you need is to go out in the cold again."

The very thought of snow sent a raft of shivers down her spine, but she couldn't abandon a man she cared about to an uncertain fate. And

she'd never been a quitter. This job was important. "I need a gun."

"The men took all of their weapons."

Angelica stalked into the kitchen. Yanking a
butcher knife from the chopping block seemed
ridiculous. If she managed to get close enough
for a knife attack, the bad guy would likely
overpower her.

But she couldn't just sit here. At the very least,
she needed to warn Spence. Back in the front
room, she zipped her Patagonia jacket that appeared lightweight but was surprisingly toasty.
"I'm going."

"I'm not strong enough to stop you." Trudy
folded her skinny arms below her breasts and
sank back on the sofa. "But I wish you'd wait."

"Until the pastor drags Spence back here by
his heels like a field-dressed deer?"

"Whatever are you talking about?"

"I think you know."

"What's gotten into you?"

The truth. She pinched her lips together to keep from blurting out accusations. Attacking Trudy wasn't going to do any good. She needed to help Spence.

On the front porch, the cold sliced through her like a blade, and she was tempted to dash back inside to wait. But the danger to Spence might be real. And she cared about him. More than friends, they had a relationship. If she closed her eyes, even for a few seconds, she felt the imprint of his embrace as he held her against his muscular chest. She remembered the deep rumble of his voice and the wood-and-leather scent of his favorite aftershave.

Looking down from the porch, she saw tracks leading from the front of the cabin toward the church next door, where lights blazed through the stained glass windows. Was she too late? Fearing the pastor and the thug had ganged up on Spence, she leaped from the porch. The snow was as deep as her knees, and she hated getting her jeans wet. But she had to warn Spence.

Slogging clumsily forward through the crisp, icy layers that glistened in the moonlight, she made her way across the front of the house to a clump of aspens and evergreens. The snow-covered boughs provided shelter from the brisk wind that swirled the icy flakes like a kaleidoscope. When she inhaled a deep breath, her lungs wheezed. She exhaled a gush of vapor. The pinpricks of frostbite returned to her toes and fingers.

She saw three men walking from the church. The pastor and Spence flanked a tall guy with floppy hair, the thug. Either he'd fooled Spence into thinking he wasn't a danger or Spence was on his side. Could he be working with the bad guys? *Trust no one.* That mantra, that perfect bit of wisdom from her dad, might also apply to Spence.

He'd said they were partners. But did she have

proof? Her sensory memories described an exquisite sexual relationship with Spence. But that didn't make him trustworthy. If she'd been able to recall with utter precision, Angelica was certain that she'd have examples of misunderstandings and mistakes. Every woman did.

Whether Spence was a sleazebag or the straight-and-true man of her dreams, he had come for her. She owed him a rescue. But how? This would have been so much easier if she'd had a gun.

She stepped out from behind the trees and waved her arms over her head. When she called out to Spence, her voice was nothing but a feral growl. When she tried to amp up the volume, her efforts vanished on the wind.

But somehow he heard the harsh sounds she was making. And he responded. Breaking into a jog, he covered the distance between them so quickly that she had to peer around him to see what the pastor and the thug were doing. Just standing there? Neither of the men moved more than a step.

Spence caught hold of her upper arms. "What are you doing outside?"

No time for talk. "Give me your gun."

"I don't think so."

"The guy you're with." She choked out the words. "And the pastor, too. They're traitors. Lock them up."

"I can explain."

"He left me to die." How could she make him understand? "He was one of the men in the van."

"I'll explain everything. For now, you've got to trust me."

"No." Her voice was firm. Her instinct was strong. She didn't owe an automatic bond of trust to him or anyone else.

"His name is Trevor," Spence said. "He's FBI, working undercover. I talked to his handler in Quantico."

"What?"

"Trevor made sure you were left alone in the van so you could escape. He didn't know what their next orders would be, and he wanted you out of danger."

She didn't understand. "Is he part of Trudy's family?"

"Her nephew."

"Why was he with those other men?"

"Undercover," Spence said. "He's working undercover."

He motioned for Clarence and the other man to join them.

Still unsure about whether she should accept this Trevor person as an undercover agent, she narrowed her gaze. It seemed awfully coincidental that Trevor and his bad guy cronies had landed near Aunt Trudy's house.

Trevor reached toward her for a handshake. "I'm sorry, Angelica."

She held back, not ready to be friends, not willing to let bygones be. She forced her voice to an almost-normal level. "Why did you choose the cabin with the green door?"

"You're going to make me work for this apology." He flashed the lopsided grin that some people might call charming. "Can we walk toward the house while I talk?"

"Not yet," she said.

"Okay, here's what happened. I was contacted by one of the bad guys, Lex Heller."

"A computer programmer," Spence said. "He's on our short list of suspects."

"He wanted me and the three other guys—Larry, Moe and Curly Joe—to take care of you." He flashed another smile, clearly his best feature. "When I say 'take care of,' I mean exactly that. We were instructed to keep you from harm. To hold you in a safe place until he contacted us."

So far, he was making sense. "Continue."

"I could see you were waking up and wanted you to have a fair chance to escape. So, I suggested the cabin near Uncle Clarence's place, and I called him to warn him."

"Which is why I never called 911," Clarence said. "I couldn't very well have the sheriff show up and take Trevor into custody."

"You lied to me," she said.

"And I'm sorry."

"What if I'd been more seriously injured?" she asked.

"I would have called an ambulance. I'd never put your life at risk," Clarence said. His blue eyes were intense. His beard puckered around his mouth. "You believe me, don't you?"

She did. "You're not a bad person, Pastor. And I understand why you didn't want to betray your nephew."

"Am I forgiven?" Trevor asked.

She grabbed his glove and gave a firm shake. "For now."

SPENCE SCOOPED ANGELICA off her feet and started to carry her toward the cabin. He liked her nearness, the intimacy and the way she felt in his arms. She was firm but not hard. No six-pack abs. No buns of steel. Her body had a feminine softness, a gift of nature that could never be achieved in a gym.

"Put me down." She lightly punched him on the chin. "What do you think you're doing?"

"Keeping you from getting your feet wet."

She stuck her legs straight out. "I have my good boots, thanks to you."

"We're almost there." He strode forward toward the cabin. Nuzzling her earlobe, he whispered, "I'm just trying to pay you back."

"I missed something." Her lips were inches from his. Her poor, tired eyes were bloodshot. Her skin was reddened and chapped. But she was still beautiful. She croaked, "You owe me?"

"In spite of frostbite, you charged out into the cold to save me."

"I should have been armed."

"I'm glad you weren't."

"Why?"

"If you'd gotten your paws on a gun, Trevor would have paid the consequences."

"Not if he followed my orders."

She didn't look anywhere near as dangerous as she actually was. Angelica qualified as a sharpshooter in pistol and in rifle, which meant her accuracy was over 90 percent. Her hand-to-hand combat skills weren't as good, and Spence was grateful for that. He didn't have to endure a Vulcan death grip every time she got riled.

As they approached the porch at the front of the cabin, she said, "It's hard for me to be authoritative when you're carrying me, but I have a few demands."

He climbed onto the porch and allowed her legs to swing down. "Shoot."

"Whenever possible, I need to be carrying a weapon."

He agreed. "If you'd been armed last night, do you think you could have gotten away from the kidnappers?"

"Don't know," she muttered. "Can't remember what happened."

"I'm with you on this. We'll have to figure out some way for both of us to carry firearms while we're inside the NORAD complex. It's a weapons-free zone."

"You're the superspy. You'll come up with something." She tapped him in the center of his chest with her forefinger. "My next demand is that you treat me like any other partner. No hugging, no carrying, no kissing…unless we're alone…and I give consent."

"That road goes both ways," he said with a grin. "So don't be rubbing up against me or making kissy faces."

"Oh, please, I don't do that."

"We'll see."

Clarence and Trevor clomped onto the porch beside them. Trevor handed her an unexpected gift.

"Your cell phone," he said.

"A thousand thanks. I never thought I'd see this again."

"It was with you when we picked you up. Don't worry, it's untraceable. I've already removed the batteries, sim card and GPS."

Spence suspected the bad guys were still tracking her, using something like his own little implanted device. Modern electronics were too tempting. Sooner or later, everyone would be wearing an array of chips for location and scanners for making payments. They'd all be blips on a giant blue screen, and there would be no need for humans at all.

Clarence opened the front door, and Trudy joyfully greeted her nephew, rushing him toward the kitchen, where she had cookies and muffins. Spence's stomach growled. When was the last time he ate? He closed the door against the cold.

Quietly, Angelica said, "My last demand is the most important. I will go to the hospital with you for tests, but I will not stay. And you're taking me with you when you talk to Lex Heller."

"Why?"

"The obvious reason," she said, "is that Lex is a computer guy. We speak the same language. Also, when he comes face-to-face with me, he'll see that his kidnapping scheme didn't slow me down."

"He might have been the one to give the orders to Trevor and his mates, but I doubt Lex hatched this scheme."

"Why not?"

As soon as he figured out that she'd been abducted, he'd been turning the event around in his head, examining the strategy. The reason for taking her was linear and simple: they wanted to find out how much she knew and to assess her level of expertise.

He wished she could remember what she'd told them or showed them. Though he wanted to believe she was clever enough to point them in a wrong direction, Angelica had been drugged and couldn't help telling the truth.

The big questions came at the end. Why had they bothered with induced amnesia? Why take that risk?

"Spence?" She gave him an adorable scowl. "It worries me when you think so hard. What's on your mind?"

"They erased your memory instead of using the more expedient solution to ensure your silence."

The scowl deepened. "Clarify."

"The best way to make sure you don't talk is to kill you."

She pointed to herself. "Not dead."

"Who's protecting you?"

He had to wonder if Daddy General Thorne was involved.

Chapter Six

This was the first time Angelica had visited this particular clinic on the outskirts of Colorado Springs. Surprising, really. While she was growing up, it felt like she'd spent time in every medical facility in the surrounding five counties. She'd broken her wrist playing on the high school lacrosse team, sprained her ankle twice, had received a total of twenty-three stitches and had sustained a series of other injuries, bumps and bruises. Her mom had always been quick to seek professional medical advice no matter how much her four kids told her they didn't need it.

Secretly, she enjoyed having Mom fuss over

her and take care of her when she was hurting. On sick days, the two of them sat in her bed together and read glossy magazines. Her twin hated when Angelica got special attention and sometimes faked an illness so she'd have her turn to cuddle with Mom and talk about clothes and makeup.

Dad was the opposite. He expected his troops and his children to be impervious to pain and injury. Angelica thought of him while she sat on the examination table having her breathing measured, her cheek swabbed and her blood drawn. There would be no tears, not now, not ever.

She owed Dad a call. He'd texted a couple of times during the day, and she needed to respond before it got too late. She hit the speed dial.

Without saying a friendly "hello," he answered, "It's about damn time you return my text messages."

"You know I'm here on business, right?"

"Computer business," he said dismissively. "It only takes a minute to call back unless you were inside NORAD where there's no cell reception. Is that where you were?"

"I can't say."

"You don't have to keep your business secret from me. We're playing for the same team, honey."

"Maybe tomorrow we'll meet for lunch. I'll call."

After she disconnected, she scowled at the phone, then looked over at Spence. "That was weird."

"How so?"

"It's not like my dad to poke into my work. He knows I work at top secret levels. And even if I tried to explain, he wouldn't get it. He's barely mastered the skills needed to use his cellphone."

She met Spence's gaze and, for a moment, got lost in the blue of his eyes. When he cleared his throat, she shook off the mesmerizing effect he had on her and continued, "Dad asked about NORAD. Why would he guess about where I was?"

Gently, he said, "Because he's your father and he cares."

"He's always been a general first." She shrugged. "Maybe retirement is catching up with him. Maybe he's going soft."

"Soft? Not the guy I met yesterday," Spence said. "General Peter Thorne gave me a steely look that said he'd kill me if I didn't treat you right."

She scoffed. "No way."

"Oh, yeah."

When the nurse came into the examination room and told her to change into the hospital gown, Angelica gave Spence a nod. "That's your cue to leave."

"Why?"

He had a point. If her memories about their relationship were correct, this wouldn't be the first time she'd disrobed in his presence. But she didn't want him to see her like this, with an overhead LED highlighting every bruise.

"I want a little privacy," she said.

"Okay, partner." He gave her shoulder a friendly pat. "I'd be looking for bruises that indicate you were hit with a stun gun or head wounds or ligature marks that would show you were forcibly restrained."

Unaccustomed to field investigating, she hadn't thought of all the forensic evidence that could be obtained from her body. She wasn't going to request a rape kit, but she needed to treat herself like a victim, taking scrapings from her fingernails and searching for fibers and potential DNA.

A twinge of embarrassment went through her. "I guess the responsible thing would be to allow a CSI to process me."

"It would be," he agreed. "But I want to play down your abduction. Plus, you've already changed clothes, and you're capable of investigating yourself."

After he left her alone in the room, she started with her fingernails, which she kept manicured, clipped short and shined up with clear polish. Likewise, the skin on her hands was smooth, massaged twice daily with a special cream her mom sent to her. Though nobody else paid much attention to her hands, Angelica liked to treat them right. She found nothing under her nails and no bruises on her knuckles. Apparently, she hadn't fought back.

She'd already had a flash of recall about being duct taped to chair arms, which meant there were no rope burns or ligatures on her wrists or ankles.

The big injury was the bruise on her right side that extended all the way to her hip. Was she slammed into a wall? Dropped from a significant height? Thrown into the trunk of a car?

The car scenario seemed most likely, especially when she discovered a double-pronged bruise typical of a stun gun on her left shoulder. Why couldn't she remember? She imagined herself standing beside the open trunk of a car. All it took to capture her was a zap from the stun gun and a hard shove.

At some point during her abduction, her regular clothing had been changed to the nondescript scrubs and sweatshirt she'd been wearing when she escaped. The conclusion was inescapable: she'd been naked in front of her enemies. Vulnerable. Helpless. She pushed the thought from her mind, not wanting to remember the shame she must have felt.

When the doctor entered, his examination seemed straightforward and simple. He found no head wound; therefore, her memory loss was not due to concussion. Rather, it was drug induced. When she asked how long it would take to get her memory back, the doctor refused to stipulate. Typically, some memories returned within a week. But some were lost forever.

Her other injuries were painful but not serious. No broken bones. No sprains. To find out what was used to drug her, they had to wait for lab tests. In the meantime, the doctor recommended pain medication and eight hours of sleep.

She refused.

Spence would have liked to leave her neatly tucked away in a hospital bed, but she insisted on coming with him to confront and interrogate Lex Heller. Side by side, they strode through the dusting of snow in the clinic's parking lot. At this lower altitude, the weather was mild with swirling flakes that twinkled in the streetlights. She climbed into the passenger seat of the rental SUV and fastened her seat belt.

Spence made one more bid. "Let me take you back to the hotel."

"So I can get kidnapped again?"

His attitude sharpened. "Is that where you were abducted? At the hotel?"

"I don't remember." Frustration weighed heavily upon her, and she exhaled in an angry huff. She couldn't give in, couldn't give up.

"I can arrange for someone to watch you."

"Easier said than done." Who could they trust? Everyone, from the FBI agents to the local cops to the computer nerds, was viewed as suspicious. "This assignment was designed for two people, you and me."

"And we've been compromised." His lips thinned. His brow pulled into a scowl. Spence didn't like losing any more than she did. "We should consider aborting our investigation."

"I vote for trying one more thing. Let's talk to Lex. We know he's involved because he hired Trevor and the goons."

"We might be able to squeeze information from him." Spence considered for a moment.

"Even if he's not central to the scheme, he might know something. Maybe he's a black hat."

Doubtful. Breaking into NORAD and stealing codes was high-level, illegal stuff, worthy of the worst, bad-guy hackers that lurked on the dark web. They were called black hats, supercriminals, and she had a hard time imagining Heller in that role. He and his crew of programmers at Peterson AFB were among the first people they met when they arrived. They'd seemed harmless.

In spite of a warrior action figure labeled Sexy Lexy in Heller's cubicle, he was asexual, an androgynous guy with a skinny chest and potbelly and stringy brown hair and greenish teeth that looked like they'd never been brushed.

Why did she remember so many details about him while so much of her mind was blank? When this amnesia wore off, she would never take her memory for granted again. She asked, "Are we going to arrest him?"

"We want him to talk, to tell us who he's working with. And we want him to hand over his computers and his codes."

"Which is why you need me to come along," she pointed out. "I speak his language."

Heller's apartment was in a bland, three-story, blond brick building with wrought iron staircases on the outside. He had the corner apartment on the first floor. Plain and homely, his place was the closest thing she could imagine to living in his mom's basement.

Spence guided the rental SUV onto the edge of the asphalt parking lot and paused. "Do you remember this place?"

She closed her eyes and concentrated. In the back of her mind, she caught a glimpse of Heller standing in the snow, wearing a faded red parka. "Not here, not this building."

"Where?" he asked. "What do you see?"

"Snow." Heavy snow blanketed the ground. "Other cars. I'm lying in the back of the van."

"What else?"

"Trevor."

Her ragged memory replayed a vision from the back of the van when Trevor met Heller. Behind them, she saw a sign for King Soopers market.

"When Heller left, Trevor got into the van with me," she said, recalling the moment. "And he told me to pretend I was unconscious. He'd help me escape."

"You're doing good," Spence said. "What else did he say?"

The memory tore into pieces and melted away. "Trevor said other stuff. He touched my shoulder. He was clearly the boss with the other guys."

"Do you remember anything before the van?"

She shook her head. "But getting that memory of Trevor is significant, right? The other memories are in there."

"And we'll find them," Spence said. "For

now, look out the front windshield. What do you make of the tire tracks in the parking lot snow?"

She unfastened her seat belt and leaned over the dashboard for a better view. "It looks like somebody pulled into a slot, and then backed out and drove away."

"Sexy Lexy had company," Spence said. "We should approach with caution."

Eagerly, she pulled the weapon he'd given her. "I'm ready."

"Put the Glock away, Quick Draw."

Though she did as he asked, Angelica was ready for payback. Last time, they grabbed her. Now it was vice versa.

Spence backed out of the apartment parking lot, circled the block and found a space on the street. In the rear of the SUV, he had bulletproof vests, which he insisted that they wear. He held out a rifle to her.

"I'm more comfortable with the handgun," she said.

"Suit yourself, princess."

In spite of the princess comment, he wasn't treating her like royalty and not making a big deal about this being her first time in the field. The training exercises at Quantico were different. Because she was a sharpshooter and had good reflexes, her scores on simulations were high. But she'd never faced real danger. Could she actually point her gun at another human being and pull the trigger?

She fell into step behind Spence and crept toward the corner apartment. All the curtains were drawn, even in the kitchen, but light spilled around the edges. She and Spence stood on either side of the dark brown door with a gold number seven attached at eye level. From inside, she heard the chatter of talk radio.

Spence rapped on the door. "FBI, open up."

There was no answer.

After he tried again, he reached down to the doorknob. Unlocked, it turned easily in his hand.

When he glanced at her, his gaze reflected calm and confidence. Though she couldn't recall details of his background, she knew that Spence handled this type of action on a regular basis. He knew what to do. She could trust him.

He shoved the door open and dashed inside. She followed.

Stepping over the threshold, she stumbled. Her steps wobbled. Her arms were weak, and her handgun felt like it weighed twenty pounds. A putrid smell wrapped around her like a filthy, rotting blanket.

Sprawled facedown across a cluttered wooden desk that took up a whole wall of his small apartment, she saw Lex Heller. He'd been shot. The back of his head was a mass of tissue, white skull and matted hair. Blood had spilled down his neck and puddled on the desk under his head. Through the streaks of blood, his unblinking eye stared at a rotary-dial, mustard-yellow, plastic telephone. Why would a high-tech guy like Lex have a landline, let alone an antiquated rotary phone?

The logical left side of her brain struggled to understand the anomaly of the old-fashioned phone. Did he use it to make untraceable calls to coconspirators? What was he up to? Who was he working with? The more emotional right brain took over as she realized that she was staring at a brutal crime. Lex Heller had been murdered. He was a young man, midtwenties, her age. And he was dead.

She swallowed hard to keep from puking. Angelica wasn't squeamish. Her dad taught her to hunt, and she butchered her own kills. Her gaze stuck on the weird angle of his shoulder blades and the curve of his jaw. She imagined him talking. What had he said to her? He had asked some weird questions about whether she and her twin ever dated the same guy.

Spence stepped in front of her, blocking her view. "We need to call this in."

"I guess we're not undercover anymore."

He took out his cell phone. "I still want to step as far out of the spotlight as possible. It's better if we aren't bogged down with a murder investigation."

"Who are you calling?"

"Ramirez seems to have gotten himself assigned to us."

She didn't like Special Agent Jay Ramirez. He was one of those macho jerks who thought a woman's place in law enforcement was fetching coffee for the men. "I'm going to look around. Don't worry—I won't touch anything."

When she turned her back, she didn't have to see the gore, but the smell followed her down the hall, beyond the tiny bathroom and into the bedroom. Heller's bed was unmade. His clothing was scattered across floor and furniture. The murderer might have been searching for something, but it was hard to tell. When it came to housekeeping, her computer-specialist friends seemed to be two distinct types: slobs or robots.

She leaned toward the robotic, with everything neatly put away in the proper place, but she knew brilliant people who lived in chaos like Lex Heller. Under a stack of papers on the dresser, she found a cell phone.

This was too good a clue to ignore. "Spence, come here."

He responded immediately. His large frame filled the bedroom door. "What is it?"

She pointed. "Can I check and see who he's been calling?"

"Do it quick. Ramirez is on his way with the cops."

In a matter of seconds, she'd bypassed Heller's security codes and passwords. The first text message she saw was a simple Returning your call. The name of the person who sent it turned her blood to ice.

"Professor Morris Fletcher." She stammered, "M-m-my first mentor."

Chapter Seven

In a brief but decisive phone conversation with his supervisor back at Quantico, Spence had been officially warned off the case. There was nothing for him to do but climb into his rental SUV and head back to the hotel. He wasn't happy about the turn of events, not a bit, and he wished there was someone else to blame for the breakdown of their assignment. But it was his fault. Their safety and their cover story had been his responsibility. He should have been more vigilant. He should have proceeded with a strategy instead of poking in dark corners and seeing what crawled out.

He seldom did well when working with a partner. Spence had never gotten high marks in "plays well with others," especially when the partner was as distracting as Angelica. He glanced over at her. She was sitting ram-rod straight in the passenger seat and staring through the windshield. Her posture and her refusal to look at him betrayed her tension, but her voice was relaxed, almost cheerful as she chattered nonstop about her old mentor, Professor Morris Fletcher.

He wouldn't have minded hearing a few words of encouragement from her. It wouldn't hurt for her to tell him that he did the best he could. Maybe she could pat him on the cheek and give him a thumbs-up for trying. Instead she launched into another story about how Professor Fletch admired Pythagoras not only for his geometry but also because he believed in reincarnation. As soon as that story ended, she started another, illustrating that Professor Fletch was wise, fun and an all-around cool guy.

Spence figured that anybody who got that much praise had something to hide. "What's his downside?"

"What do you mean?"

"Addictions, womanizing, gambling." He could have listed a dozen more potential problems for the fantastic Fletch. Nobody was perfect. When he got right down to it, Spence was a glass-half-empty guy.

"Why does there have to be a downside?"

"Come on, angel, there's got to be something wrong with the guy. We just learned that Professor Fletch was in communication with a traitor, a man who was murdered."

She turned toward him. The glow from the dashboard highlighted her cheekbones and the wisps of black hair that fell across her forehead. "It almost sounds like you're jealous."

"Of Professor Fletch? A pudgy little guy

with a ZZ Top beard?" he scoffed. "Give me a break."

"How do you know about his beard?" she asked suspiciously.

"I looked him up on my phone while we were waiting for the troops to arrive at Heller's place. When you saw his name, you got so…excited."

"And you got jealous," she said with a hint of smugness. "Well, you can relax. Professor Fletch isn't my type. He's gay."

"And he's also a suspect."

"Until you have evidence, I don't believe that." She turned her head and looked out the passenger-side window facing the hotel. "I wish you'd trust my judgment. Maybe I can't read people as well as you, but I trust Professor Fletch."

As far as he could tell, her basis for trust was nothing more than fond memories of an old professor. That wasn't enough to clear Fletch from suspicion. He ought to lecture her about the need for separating emotion from investigation, reminding her that many sociopaths are charming. But he didn't want to make her mad. She was more than a partner. Angelica was his girlfriend, and he meant to treat her that way for the rest of their so-called assignment in Colorado Springs.

"You're staying in my room tonight," he said.

"I have no problem with that. You have a suite, right?"

"And a hot tub. I'm paying for the upgrade."

"Dibs," she said. "I get first soak."

When they checked in, they'd taken separate rooms to keep up the appearance of propriety. No point in continuing that charade. Anybody who didn't know they were a couple would catch on pretty fast.

"You know," he said, "if you'd been sleeping in my bed last night, we might have avoided the whole kidnapping thing."

"I thought of that." She shook her head. "I still

don't remember what happened, but it seems likely that I was lured from the hotel."

He'd picked apart the bits of information he had about the kidnapping and put them back together a dozen times. The method used to take her seemed simple. "After we left your parents' house, I had to go to FBI headquarters for a meeting with SSA Sheeran. She picked me up."

"And I drove back to the hotel. That's when I must have been taken from the parking lot."

Though he wasn't a believer in coincidence, he couldn't blame the local branch of the FBI for drawing him out. The meeting with Supervisory Special Agent Raquel Sheeran had been scheduled before he left Quantico. He'd thought she was the only one who knew the real purpose of their investigation, but Sheeran had obviously told Ramirez and another agent named Tapper.

After Angelica had been abducted, Spence's behavior had been so lax that he was embarrassed. Without verifying, he had accepted a phony text saying that she was going to stay at her parents' house. Naive as a schoolboy, he had believed it, decided to give her some space. Then he got another text in the early morning telling him she had a lead, and another saying she was inside NORAD, where cell phone service was pretty much nonexistent. He should have known she wouldn't go inside without him, should have suspected. But he'd been blind. He hadn't started searching for her until after ten in the morning.

In the parking lot outside the six-story, stucco hotel, he drove slowly between the rows of vehicles. Last night, it hadn't been snowing, but the lot looked much the same. He hoped she'd see something that would spark a memory.

"You told me," she said, "that when we got back to the hotel, you had a technique that would help me remember. Were you talking about hypnosis?"

"It's more like relaxation."

"Good. Hypnosis doesn't work for me. I'm too resistant."

He wasn't surprised. She liked to know exactly what was going on at all times, demanded to be in control. These memory lapses had to be driving her crazy. "We can start right now."

"Okay."

"You've got to stop talking. Then, lean back against the seat and open up your mind."

"This is never going to work."

He could tell that she was too tense and restless to allow anything from her subconscious to come through. She wiggled in the seat. Her eyelids flickered. And her fingers twitched. Attempting a relaxation exercise now was useless.

"On second thought, maybe we should wait," he said, "until we're in the room."

"I might do better after I've had a shower. And something to eat."

It was going to take some serious quiet time

for her to be in the right mood, but getting her there might be fun. He looked forward to opening her mind and giving her the peace she needed to remember.

IN THE HOTEL, they went directly to his suite on the fourth floor. Angelica had intended to take a shower or soak away the last frigid trace of hypothermia in a hot tub, but she didn't make it that far. Halfway across the bedroom, the king-size bed beckoned, and she succumbed, flopping across the pillows as she kicked off her boots. Sleep might be the best way to reset her memory, similar to rebooting a computer. At least that was what she told herself as her eyelids closed.

When she sank into slumber, she dreamed of fat, white snowflakes tumbling silently through the upper branches of tall pine trees, like confetti in a snow globe. There was no cold, no wind, no chill at all. This was one of those dreams when she was aware of dreaming and watching herself. Snow geese with glistening feathers swooped across the sky, pulling a golden chariot. Had she seen this in a movie? The charioteer was a powerfully built snow god with a halo of unruly blond hair and piercing pale eyes. It was Spence. She took the time to study him as he approached and disembarked.

Of course, she knew that Special Agent Spence Malone had never dressed like this in real life. As if he'd ever wear etched gold cuffs on his muscular wrists? Or a pale toga that flipped open and offered a view of his chest and six-pack abs?

Dream Spence coiled an arm around her waist and pulled her close. Though she couldn't really smell anything in a dream, the odor of afternoon rain and pheromones—whatever those smelled like—scented the air.

"Are you all right?" It was his real voice, not the rumblings of a snow god.

"Fine," she murmured.

"You were making weird noises," he said. "Are you hungry?"

In her dream, she was ready to lock lips, but her hand dropped to her belly. Real-life Angelica wanted food. "Onion rings."

"Good, that's what I ordered, and steak."

"Don't care."

She dived back into her dream, closed her eyes, puckered up and prepared to be ravaged by a brazen snow god. His firm lips brushed across hers and moved away, leaving her craving more. The next taste was deeper. And then his mouth pressed harder, and his tongue plunged into her mouth.

Excitement stirred her blood. An impatient moan rose in her throat, and she realized...*I'm not dreaming.* The real Spence lay beside her on the king-size bed. His expert kisses were driving her wild.

She wanted him, but not now, not yet. There

were questions to be answered, memories to be reinstated. Her hands pushed against his chest, holding him at a distance. Like the snow god, he'd stripped off his shirt. The muscles beneath his warm, supple flesh were firm. This wasn't the first time she'd thought of how big and strong he was. That fact didn't count as a regained memory. It was merely an observation.

"Did you mention room service?" she asked.

"I made the call just before the kitchen closed at 1:00 a.m."

She wasn't sure what time they'd gotten to the room. "How long have I been sleeping?"

"A couple of hours." He ran a hand across his bare chest. "I took a shower and made some calls."

"And why did you wake me?"

"Well, there were the weird noises."

She was getting a whole different vibe from him. Not a romantic snow god or a tough undercover agent, he had transformed into Spence the boyfriend. "You thought maybe we should eat before we…you know."

He grinned. "Have mind-blowing sex?"

"You're awfully sure of yourself."

"I have reason to be."

She barked a laugh. Spence might be the hottest, sexiest man she'd ever met, but he was also funny. And she found his sense of humor to be almost as appealing as his gorgeous body.

When he made a grab for her, she jumped off the bed, not wanting to start something they couldn't finish before the food arrived. She announced, "I'm going to clean up."

The hot tub was enticing, but she settled for the extra-large shower with four different heads. Within a few minutes, she had the steam churning inside the glass stall. The soothing heat penetrated all the way to her core.

She wondered if she and Spence had ever bathed together. It seemed likely, but she didn't exactly recall. There were other gaps in her memories of him. Their first meeting was hazy, and their first kiss.

Amnesia had taken a toll, which was not necessarily a negative thing. Without a record of those sensual memories, she could experience them, again, for the first time. It would feel like being a virgin again. As the hot water sluiced between her breasts and down her belly, she imagined his touch. His hands were huge, but she knew he'd be gentle. Why couldn't she remember? Did they sleep with the lights on or off?

She rinsed her hair, turned off the shower jets and grabbed a towel. She recalled their night at the Arena Theater and the aftermath with champagne and roses. That night, they'd made all kinds of passionate love, and she remembered feeling good even though the specifics were hazy.

Did her amnesia reach six months into her past? Or did that only apply to memories of

Spence? There might be a reason she didn't remember him.

She slipped into her blue-and-gray-striped nightgown. All cleaned and combed, she felt like she'd regained some of her self-control. It was time to make sense of her amnesia. Why did she remember some things and forget about others?

It seemed likely that she would block out unpleasant memories. The moment when she was grabbed wasn't clear in her mind, and that fit the pattern. She didn't want to remember her failure in her first field assignment. Her high hopes for becoming more than a desk jockey had crashed when the bad guys lured her and abducted her.

But there were other negative moments that she recalled. She remembered the horrible sense of vulnerability when her abductors had changed her clothing. The thought of that humiliation flushed her cheeks with embarrassment. Being duct taped to a chair was another incident she didn't want to recall, but there it was in her mind.

She'd also like to erase the gruesome image of Lex Heller with the back of his head blown off. But that wasn't under the purview of her amnesia.

Spence was there before she'd been drugged and after. He was central. She hated to think there was a reason she was blanking memories of him from her mind. Was he hiding something?

Using the hotel's gift supply, she applied lotion to her hands and arms. *I'm being ridiculous.* She had to trust Spence. He was her partner.

When she entered the front room, she saw the room service cart parked by the table. The scent of grilled meat spiked her hunger. When she lifted the round silver cover, she saw a fat, juicy T-bone with tomato and lettuce and a whole plate of onion rings. Before she could say anything, Spence signaled for her to be quiet.

Wearing nothing but a pair of sweatpants, he tiptoed across the room toward the door. In his left hand, he held a bottle of champagne. His Glock was in his right. A few feet away from the door, he leaned down and picked up a thin cord, the type of equipment used with fiber optics to spy beyond locked doors.

Spence set down the champagne. He coiled the cord around his hand and gave a sharp yank.

From outside the door, there was a thud.

Spence whipped open the door and aimed his handgun at a plump, bearded man.

"Professor Fletch."

Chapter Eight

If the consequences of the NORAD hack hadn't held the potential for nuclear disaster, if she hadn't been abducted, if Lex Heller hadn't been murdered, Angelica might have laughed. Outside their hotel room door, a perfect nerd tableau had formed. Her favorite mentor, Professor Fletcher, adjusted the ear flaps on his striped, knit cap and twiddled his beard. A skinny young guy with a man bun sat on the carpet and typed frantically into a laptop. In spite of the snow outside, he wore only a thermal long-sleeved turtleneck under a Hawaiian-print shirt decorated with flamingos and macaws. A third nerd, who looked familiar, was on his knees with his butt sticking up in the air and his nose pressed to the reader for the fiber-optic device that he'd tried to slip under their door.

Standing opposite these three was Spence, wearing only a pair of loose-fitting gray sweatpants. In one hand, he held a Glock. A magnum of champagne was in the other fist. His testosterone level more than tripled that of the nerds.

In a strange way, the contrast represented the different sides of her life. She would always be the tomboy who had majored in math and graduated to being a full-fledged computer hacker. But she was also a woman with passions who dedicated herself to solving cyber crime and believed in doing the right thing for herself, her family and her nation. Though not the female version of Spence, she was a capable partner— as long as they were on the same side. The jury was still out on whether or not she could trust him completely.

Clearly out of patience, he glared at the threesome and growled, "Get inside. Shut the door."

They scrambled to do as he said. While two of them alighted on the sofa, Professor Fletch marched toward her with his arms held out for a big hug. He ripped off his cap, releasing a frizzy cloud of steely-gray hair. She thought he was smiling. With the beard, it was hard to tell.

"My, my, my, Angelica, aren't you a sight for these tired old eyes?"

Oh, no, you don't. She wasn't going to let him breeze in here, pretending nothing had happened. "Stop right there, Professor. It would have been easier to see me if you weren't sliding cameras under my door."

"I didn't want to disturb you."

"Don't be ridiculous."

In the past, she'd thought his silliness was charming and amusing—a refreshing change from people who took themselves too seriously. But there was a time to put aside the fun and games. Murder made this the right time to focus.

"Angelica, listen to me." He sounded a pleading note. "I came to help you."

"How?" Was he trying to give her actual evidence? "Do you have information?"

"Nothing you don't already know."

"Are you sure about that? How do you know what I do or don't know?"

"Think for a moment."

The answer was clear. The professor had trained her. He was a talented hacker who sometimes monitored the police radio or cut into their computer systems. As far as she knew, he steered clear of breaking into the FBI computers, but she wouldn't put it past him. "Oh, my God, what do you know?"

"I'm sure your skills surpass anything I might have taught you. I'm here to offer my services," he said with an expansive grin, "and the use of my equipment and technology."

Spence gestured with his gun. "Professor, join your friends on the sofa."

"I'm happy, delighted, thrilled to cooperate."

She'd never before noticed what tiny steps Professor Fletch took. Had he been ill? Was this something new? She had to wonder if he'd been toying with her when he offered his help. He could be trying to use their former mentor-student relationship to direct the investigation. But why? She couldn't imagine Fletch being involved in a plot to hack into missile launch technology. He was opposed to the proliferation of nuclear weaponry.

Her gaze drifted to the room service cart where dinner awaited under silver-covered lids. The smell of deep-fried onion rings was driving her crazy.

Spence slapped his gun in her hand. "Keep an eye on these three while I get zip ties."

Holding them at gunpoint seemed excessive, but she didn't argue. They might look nerdy, but that didn't mean they weren't dangerous. The unwanted vision of Lex Heller's death flashed across her mind, and she forced herself to erase the bad memory of blood and gore. Positioned in front of the sofa, she remained standing with the Glock braced two-handed in front of her.

The guy who had been operating the fiber-optic device unzipped his parka and took it off. His T-shirt said: I Read Your Email.

"You," she snapped, "don't make another move."

"Would you really shoot?"

"Don't push me." Her gaze was hard enough to cut through his thick, horn-rimmed glasses and fierce enough to make him wriggle away from her on the sofa.

"But you know me," he said. "I'm Bo Lambert. I work at the base with Lex Heller."

"That's enough. Please be quiet." *What's*

wrong with me? I shouldn't have said please. It wasn't easy to be intimidating while wearing a striped nightgown with a terry-cloth hotel bathrobe hanging from her shoulders. And she'd made herself even less scary by being polite.

"There's no need for the gun," Professor Fletch said.

"Quiet," she muttered.

"Angelica, we're on the same side."

"Quiet!" she said a bit more loudly.

"There's a need for communication." Fletch looked to his two companions. "Am I right?"

"QUIET!" She swept the Glock in an arc. For a nanosecond, she considered shooting them all and sitting down to eat her onion rings before they got cold. "PLEASE. BE. QUIET."

Three sets of eyeballs focused on her, waiting for her to make the next move. Did they already know their friend had been murdered? How would they react? Who could have told them?

Angelica kept her mouth shut. Spence was

the expert when it came to interrogation, but she wondered if these three nerds might be an exception. They could identify with her and, therefore, might be more willing to talk to one of their kind.

The guy with the Hawaiian shirt and man bun raised his hand. His scrawny frame pressed tightly against Professor Fletch, and she wondered if they were a couple.

She glared at him. "What?"

"This."

He swiveled his laptop to face her. There was a photograph of Lex Heller, dead at his desk. Startled by the horrific image, she held her breath and tensed her muscles to keep from dropping the gun. This guy with the flamingo shirt was her age, possibly younger, and yet so callous.

"What's your name?" she asked.

"Dunne, Howie Dunne."

Easy to remember; Dunne rhymed with bun. "Where did you get that picture?"

"You should be answering the questions," he said. "How could you let this happen to Lex? He should have been under your protection."

Spence came back into the room. He wore jeans, a black FBI T-shirt and an angry expression. Jaw clenched, he leaned down to stare at the laptop. "What time did you get this picture?"

"I don't have to answer your questions," Dunne said. "I want a lawyer."

"Me, too," said Bo Lambert. "My cousin is a lawyer. He could be here in ten minutes."

"I don't have time for this." Spence took the laptop and handed it to her with a simple instruction. "Get all the info you can off this computer."

She knew the drill. "Consider it done."

Dunne bounced to his feet to protest. Before he could take one single step, Spence shoved him back down onto the sofa. "Give me your hands."

"No." Dunne stuck out his pointy, unshaven chin. "You can't make me. And your girlfriend can't break into my computer."

"I regret," Professor Fletch said, "to inform you that Angelica Thorne was one of my best students. She can do anything she wants with your laptop, maybe teach it to dance and whistle the theme from *Close Encounters of the Third Kind*."

"Thanks for the validation," she said.

Spence stepped between them, ending their moment of mutual admiration. "Now, Professor Fletcher, show me your hands."

The professor complied, and Spence slipped on the zip ties. He did the same with Lambert, and then he turned to Dunne. "You're next."

His righteous anger was fading fast, but he made an effort. "You won't get any fingerprints other than mine from the computer. I wiped it down, even the keys."

"Who are you protecting?" Spence asked.

"None of your business."

Spence growled, "Hands."

"Don't you have to read me my rights?"

"You're not under arrest...not yet, anyway."

"You should cooperate, Dunne. Give him what he wants," Professor Fletch said. "A young man has been killed. I want to know why."

Spence fastened the zip ties on Dunne, took a step back and sat in the overstuffed chair beside the sofa. As he took the Glock from her, he said in a low voice, "Take the room service cart to the bedroom. I suggest you go in there, close the door, figure out the computer and eat the onion rings while they're still hot."

"And what are you going to do?"

"I already put in a call to SSA Sheeran. She's coming over to take these three into custody for questioning."

"But you have more interrogation experience," she protested. "You could—"

"Until tomorrow, you and I are officially off the case."

As far as she was concerned, that decision amounted to a big, fat pile of bureaucratic baloney. Dropping the cover story about checking systems at NORAD was smart. Nobody had believed them, anyway, which was why she'd been kidnapped.

She'd be glad when they could present themselves as an investigative team with teeth who had come to Colorado Springs to rip into cyber crime. As investigators, they could make demands, have access to forensic information and perform interrogations. They had control—as soon as their bosses at Quantico gave the okay.

Turning on her heel, she set a course for the bedroom. Inside with the door closed, she exhaled a huge sigh and let down her guard. Still tired in spite of her nap, she sank onto the bed, with the room service cart beside her and the laptop on the bedspread in front of her. *Which to do first?* Eating would give her an energy boost, but she was anxious to get started on Dunne's computer.

She lifted the silver lid on the onion rings, snatched one and popped it into her mouth. *Yum, tasty.* With her other hand, she entered codes that would bypass the computer's passwords. Multitasking came easily.

The lightly greasy onion ring made her mouth happy. But that simple pleasure was nothing compared to the electric jolt that charged through her veins when her fingertips touched the keys of the laptop. Working at the computer was something she remembered, 100 percent. Her memory was coming back. A light flashed on in her brain. Neural disconnects were mended and faulty synapses crackled to life.

She closed her eyelids and tried to remember what had happened yesterday. They arrived at Peterson AFB and were escorted to the area where Heller and Lambert worked. Though the gist of their conversation wasn't clear in her mind, she recalled being convinced that their interpretation of the threat was correct: a hacker had broken through firewalls and viral protection to access NORAD's missile data. There hadn't been an actual attempt to launch. The access was worrisome enough.

Eyes still closed, she tried to recall dinner with Mom and Dad. She could almost hear her dad greeting them, could almost feel her mom's embrace and smell her familiar lavender perfume. In her memory, she tilted her head to the left and looked for Spence. Shouldn't he be standing beside her? Shouldn't she be introducing him, carefully phrasing her words to let her parents know he was important? Was he?

Her visions of being in bed with Spence were vivid. But day-to-day life was a blur. How important was he? *I mean, really.* If he was "the one," the man she was supposed to be with, why wasn't she wearing a diamond?

She needed to set her mind right about him and her relationship with him. But first, she needed to decode and decrypt Dunne's computer before SSA Sheeran arrived and confiscated this bit of evidence.

Blindly, she tapped away at the keyboard, following decryption patterns that were so familiar she didn't need to see the keys. Her sensory memory was returning. Details emerged more clearly. Without thinking, she typed a series of codes and binary sequences she'd discovered when initially investigating the hack back at Quantico.

She opened her eyes, blinked and stared at the screen in front of her. Most of her work was familiar, but there was an odd bit that she couldn't explain: Y75110. A license plate number? Digits on an ID badge? An activation code? If it activated something, what was it?

There was more to learn from this computer. Typing with one hand and eating with the other, she explored, delving beyond the mundane emails, processes, tools and systems. The first—and most obvious—anomaly she discovered was that the computer didn't belong to Dunne. It came from Peterson AFB and could be traced to the department where Heller and Bo Lambert worked.

She reached for another onion ring and realized there were no more. Without noticing, she'd eaten the whole plateful. Moving on with her late dinner, she went for straight protein. She cut off a bite of steak and chewed while pondering the significance of the computer's provenance. It was only a few months old and hadn't been activated on a regular basis. Downloads were what she'd expect for a general office computer. No other photos were stored. She couldn't tell if this laptop belonged to one particular person in the office or was passed from desk to desk.

Had it been at Heller's house when he was killed? She checked the time stamp of the grisly photo. It had been taken forty minutes before she and Spence found the body, which was, according to the local police, approximately the time of death. Had the murderer taken the photograph? Why? And why did Dunne have the computer?

She sliced off another bite of steak and opened the file for emails. The current file was clear. Only about fifty had been deleted, mostly office memos that were sent to every computer in the department.

While searching the computer's history, she discovered a pattern. Three weeks ago, there'd been a fast and heavy exchange of emails with a sender using the name: C4ICBM. That code was more than a little bit ominous. C4 was a plastic explosive, and ICBM stood for Intercontinental Ballistic Missile. The nightmare scenario for their investigation would be to uncover a plan for launching those missiles and setting off the warheads.

Again, she squeezed her eyes closed and tried to remember what had happened while she'd been abducted. She might have overheard the plan or caught a glimpse of something dangerous. An unauthorized missile launch was unthinkable. Her research on that possibility had concluded that the strategic air defense systems were impregnable and unhackable. Even if they could be hacked, there were fail-safe measures in place to abort the action before the missiles were airborne.

But nothing was impossible. She clicked on one of the mysterious emails to open it. The bland conversation referred to a family reunion that might take place in Dallas or Seattle or Seoul. Why was South Korea mentioned in the same breath with Dallas and Seattle? What was the connection in those far-flung locations? The sixteenth of November—three days from today—was mentioned as the time for the reunion.

She read the sign-off line aloud. "Office1116."

Chapter Nine

Spence credited his effectiveness as an interrogator to a combination of training and instinct. Growing up at the ragged edges of the foster care system, he learned early on that information was power. The more details he had, the better off he was. Knowing who to trust meant the difference between scoring a bottle of gin and getting blamed for stealing cigarettes from the corner liquor store. He developed his instincts. At a glance, he could sense when somebody was lying or hiding something.

Convincing the other kids to spill their hard-won secrets was easier because of his size. By the time he was in sixth grade, he had almost reached his full adult height, big enough that he didn't need to hit anybody to be threatening. He'd loom over another kid, standing in silence and watching until they couldn't wait to give him whatever he wanted.

His FBI training taught him more subtle techniques designed to intimidate, confuse and enrage a suspect. He used every growl, smile and twist on the three miscreants who sat side by side on the sofa. Thus far, his efforts proved futile.

Lambert and Dunne both refused to talk. Bo was scared speechless and just wanted to consult his cousin, the lawyer. Though Dunne had just as much fear, he kept it locked inside a supposedly hard-boiled exterior that didn't fool anybody. It took a special breed of tough guy to pull off a man bun and Hawaiian flamingo shirt. Dunne didn't fit that mold.

The closest Spence came to a conversation

was getting Professor Fletch to open up about Angelica's parents. He and the general had always been on the same page about encouraging her work in math and computers. Fletch was also friendly with Pastor Clarence and Trudy, not surprising given that they were close to the same age and social strata. The professor had a little cabin in the mountains and occasionally attended the pastor's church, where his wife directed an excellent choir.

Spence was pinching himself to stay awake when Angelica emerged from the bedroom. Immediately, the room got brighter. There was a bounce in her step. Her green eyes flashed. He knew that she'd discovered useful evidence.

After warning the threesome not to move, he picked up his Glock and guided Angelica toward the small kitchenette at the far end of the suite where he could still keep an eye on his suspects. He placed his gun on the countertop and turned toward her. "What did you find?"

"Number one," she said, "this laptop comes from Peterson AFB, from the decryption unit where Heller and Lambert both worked. The computer wasn't assigned to an individual."

"Either of them could have used the laptop at work."

"Or taken it home."

As could any other person who happened to waltz through their offices where security was low-key. "The real question is, who took the picture of Heller? Was it Lambert?"

"He doesn't seem like the type who goes looking for trouble."

Spence agreed. Bo Lambert was an ostrich not a peacock—or a flamingo like Dunne. When they identified the person who snapped the photo, they'd be close to finding the murderer. "It could be anybody. What do you call that? An infinite number of variables?"

"Close enough."

She tossed her head, and a wing of black hair

fell across her forehead. The cedar scent of the hotel's shampoo mingled with her natural intoxicating fragrance.

"Are you sniffing me?" She shot him a grin. "I stink like onion rings, right? And steak?"

"You smell real damn good." He inhaled deeply. "I'm not talking about food."

Her gaze linked with his. They connected for only an instant but the contact was intense. His desire to touch her manifested in gliding his hand along the countertop until his fingertips were only a few centimeters from her arm.

She froze, not moving closer or putting distance between them. "There was only that one photo, taken near the time Heller was murdered."

"How do you know that for sure?"

"Time stamp," she said. "It hasn't been doctored. Nothing else has been erased."

These details were useful but fairly obvious. "What else?"

"Emails." She set the laptop on the counter and clicked a few computer keys to bring up the file. "It's mostly office junk mail, but you can see that a back-and-forth correspondence started about three weeks ago."

"Which is when SSA Sheeran contacted Quantico with her suspicions," he said. She'd been operating on information given to her by the cyber coders who perceived a hack on the weapons systems. "They couldn't track the intruder, couldn't find any changes in the systems or the firewall protections."

"Window-shopping," she said.

That was how she'd explained the hack when first presented with the data. The hacker had slipped inside, checked things out and left without attempting to manipulate the system.

"Tell me about this chatter," he said.

"The methodology is primitive, similar to exchanging coded messages during Cold War spying." She pointed to the screen. "The name of the correspondent is C4ICBM."

"Dynamite," he muttered under his breath.

"No, it's C4."

"Same difference. Not that a nuclear warhead attached to a rocket isn't enough to get my attention."

"The sender has identified him or herself as Office1116. The emails appear to be talking about a family reunion. Three cities are mentioned—Seattle, Dallas and Seoul."

No connection among those locations popped to mind. Seattle and Dallas might be approximately the same distance from Peterson AFB in Colorado Springs. But Seoul, why Seoul? He glanced at the sofa where the three nerds fidgeted nervously. SSA Sheeran would be here at any moment to pick them up. If he was going to get information from them, it had to be now. "I should get back to our suspects."

"Wait." She opened an email and pointed to

an odd sequence. "Do you see that? Y75110? Do you know what it stands for?"

"Not a clue."

He pivoted and stalked toward the sofa. Not bothering with the other two, he zeroed in on Lambert, grabbed a chair from the table and swung it around to face the sofa. Unless he swiveled his head all the way to the side, Lambert couldn't avoid seeing Spence. Their knees were almost touching.

"I've got a problem," Spence said in cool, low voice. "You knew about the laptop. It came from your office area."

"I…I…I didn't notice it," he stammered.

"Here's the deal, Lambert, you should want me to be your friend. Supervisory Special Agent Sheeran is on her way. When she takes you into custody, you're looking at a world of hurt."

"What do you mean?" His weasel face twisted into a knot. Using both hands, he pushed his wire-frame glasses up on his nose.

"For starters, you'll lose your job. The FBI will contact every person you know—former instructors like Professor Fletch, other employers, girlfriends and your family."

His eyes filled with tears. "My dad?"

"Mom, Dad and grandparents," Spence said, driving his point home. "If you're lucky, you won't be in prison too long."

"What do I have to do?"

"Cooperate, starting now. Have you seen that laptop before tonight?"

He nodded. "It's been in the department. I've never used it. I stick with my own computer."

"What about Heller?"

Lambert hunched his shoulders. Shivering, he stared down at his fingers and plucked at the zip ties that fastened his wrists. "I can't say."

"You don't have to be afraid."

"I'm not."

"Heller can't hurt you."

After a sidelong glance at the two people who

sat beside him, Lambert whispered, "He asked me to help."

"What did Heller ask you to do?"

"He said he'd pay me five thousand bucks for a few hours' work."

"Tell me about this work." Spence felt like reaching down Lambert's throat and dragging the words from him. "Some kind of software or computer coding?"

"Not that." His chin lifted. Through his thick lenses, he scanned the room until he saw Angelica. "Heller said we'd be helping you. That's why I even listened to him for even one minute. I wanted you to notice me, to remember me. I was two years behind you in school. We had classes together. You were one of the first girls I had a crush on."

Moving to stand beside Spence, she masked her reaction well, keeping her expression and her voice calm. "I'm sorry if it seemed like I was ignoring you. You've changed."

"You haven't." A hint of a smile twisted his thin, pale lips. "A beautiful angel."

"Not really, I was more of a devil than an angel. Tell him, Professor."

Fletch cleared his throat. "She hasn't always been a good girl but certainly isn't devilish. That's her twin sister."

She leaned down and gazed directly into Lambert's eyes. "What did Heller want you to do?"

"I looked up to you. And now, you're at NSA investigating cyber crime. You're living the dream."

"Help me, Bo. We need to find the murderer."

He gave a decisive nod. "I got a call from Heller around midnight last night. He wanted me to come to his apartment and pick him up. That's when he promised the five grand and said I'd be helping you."

"Did you go?"

"I did. It was a lapse in judgment on my part."

Spence would call it more than a lapse. In following Heller's instructions, Lambert had taken a vacation from his conscience and his sense of right and wrong.

"When I got there," Lambert said, "Heller was babbling about conspiracy theories and fortunes to be made. I turned down his offer of money to do something crazy but I agreed to let him use my car. It's an SUV and drives better in the mountains."

Spence was beginning to piece together a narrative. They knew, from what Trevor had told them, that Heller had been responsible for delivering Angelica to the thugs at a mountain location. Heller had been driving Lambert's vehicle, which meant that he not only had an SUV that handled well in snow but Lambert's car would be caught on any surveillance cameras.

"So dumb!" Lambert cursed himself. "I never should have gotten involved."

"Don't blame yourself," Professor Fletcher

said. "You were trying to help your friend. And you didn't break any laws."

"Heller was talking crazy, said I shouldn't have called him on my cell, only landlines. We could escape to a nonextradition country, change our identities or fake our deaths."

Fletch nodded sympathetically as he combed his fingers through his beard. "Now and then, we've all considered such fascinating possibilities."

Dunne finally spoke up. "I have."

"Do tell," Fletcher said.

"Someday, if you're real nice, I'll show you my collection of fake IDs."

"That's not me," Lambert said. "I'm just trying to do the right thing."

Spence put him back on track. "How did you get your car back?"

"Heller didn't even have the common courtesy to bring it to my house." He adjusted his glasses. "I don't like speaking ill of the dead, but Lex Heller could be difficult."

"Bo called me," the professor said. "He sounded agitated, disturbed. I sent Dunne to pick him up."

"Yeah, yeah," Dunne said. "I got to Lambert's place at three fifteen, and we drove to Heller's apartment. Bo's car was parked in the lot."

"But Heller's little Honda was gone."

Now that they'd decided to talk, the three suspects were chirping like hungry baby birds. Spence held up his hand for quiet. "Did Heller answer the door?"

"Nope," said Dunne, "and we knew he wasn't home because the curtains were open and we couldn't see anybody inside."

Spence exchanged a glance with Angelica. When they had arrived at the apartment, all the blinds were drawn and curtains closed. He asked Lambert, "Did you check out your car?"

"I most certainly did. Heller went approximately forty-three miles and used a third of a tank of gas, which he did not replace. I can't give you details of his destination because my vehicle isn't equipped with the GPS tracking system."

"Did you speak to Heller again?"

"I was so mad at him."

"We all were," Dunne said.

Lambert frowned, shook his head and looked down. "I can't believe he's dead. I should have done something, tried to convince him to go to the police. Instead, I was worried about my stupid car. After we left the apartment, Dunne and I went to the professor's house and stayed for dinner."

"Hey," Dunne said, "that's our alibi. We had dinner together. We've got nothing to worry about."

"Is that true?" Lambert asked.

Spence didn't reply; these were intelligent men who could figure it out for themselves.

"Sure, it's true," Dunne said. "When we were at Heller's apartment, we looked in the windows, and there were no dead bodies. The rest of the day, we were together."

Lambert exhaled heavily. "I can't believe we need alibis. That doesn't seem right."

"Because it's not," Fletch said. "You're not off the hook quite yet."

"Why not?" Dunne demanded.

"You can't alibi each other," Spence logically explained, "if you're suspected of working together to commit the murder."

Dunne's bubble burst. He slouched backward while Lambert leaned forward, resting his elbows on his thighs.

Spence rose from his chair, went to the kitchenette, picked up the computer and brought it back to the sofa. He placed it on the coffee table. After a brief debate with himself about whether to display the photo, he decided not to. This would be a closed-casket interrogation.

He took a step back. "How did you get this computer?"

"I'll explain." The professor cleared his throat before continuing. "After dinner as Bo was leaving, he found it tucked inside the screen door on my covered porch. The time was a little after eight. When we saw the photo, we panicked."

Spence had only one more question: "Why?"

"I was afraid that someone was trying to frame me," the professor said. "Believe it or not, I have enemies."

"Closed-minded idiots," Dunne muttered.

"You're no genius," Lambert said. "You wiped off all the fingerprints and wanted to pitch the laptop off Pikes Peak."

"Which would have been wrong," Fletch said. "We needed to contact the authorities. That's when I remembered that Angelica was in town. I knew she had an important job with national security and hoped she'd help us."

Spence wasn't sure how much of their story

he believed. Some parts were undoubtedly true, but one aspect didn't make sense no matter how he looked at it. *Why had the murderer taken a photo of his victim, and then delivered it to Professor Fletcher?*

The door to their suite crashed open. Supervisory Special Agent Raquel Sheeran charged through and took a shooter's stance, holding her gun in a two-fisted grip. Her long, red mane tumbled halfway down her back. He'd forgotten how dynamic she was.

Behind her were Ramirez and Special Agent Mike Tapper. Almost in unison, they announced their presence. "Federal Agents."

Chapter Ten

Amnesia or not, Angelica knew she'd seen that woman before. In high-heeled boots, SSA Raquel Sheeran stood an inch shy of six feet tall, which made it easy for her to look down her nose at mere mortal females. Her FBI windbreaker had been tailored to show her nipped-in waist and well-rounded bottom while skinny jeans molded lovingly to her superlong legs.

In addition to her intimidating physical attributes, her husky voice resonated with a commanding tone. Most definitely an alpha personality, she was aggressive, tough and competitive. Grudgingly, Angelica had to acknowledge that Sheeran's accomplishments were worthy of applause. Becoming a supervisor in a field dominated by men was impressive. How many individuals had SSA Sheeran had thrown off the ladder to claw her way to the next rung higher?

Raquel approached Angelica for a handshake. "Pleased to meet you."

"It's not the first time." In spite of the residual soreness of near hypothermia, Angelica matched the other woman's overstrong grasp with a hard squeeze of her own. "A few years ago, we were both part of a group that toured inside Cheyenne Mountain."

"Why would you take the tour? You're a local."

"Showing one of my cousins the sights—I never missed an excuse to dive inside the facility. I've been fascinated by NORAD ever since I was a kid and called on Christmas Eve to check Santa's progress."

She'd pointed to the NORAD Santa Tracker as proof when her cynical twin sister quit believing. Angelica recalled the distant past clearly when she'd cited radar images for an unidentified flying sleigh and eight reindeer. And there had been the annual phone call to the jolly old elf, himself.

As a grown-up, she'd volunteered to answer the Santa phones on the twenty-fourth. Pretending to be Mrs. Claus, she'd wish the kids a happy holiday and tell them to get to bed so Santa could visit.

"The Santa Tracker," Sheeran said with disdain. "It might be good public relations but kind of a scam."

"And I suppose you don't believe in unicorns, leprechauns and the tooth fairy."

"I suppose not."

If Sheeran wanted to live in a world without magic, that was her choice. And it wasn't surprising. The way Angelica remembered the tour when they'd first met, Sheeran had been preoccupied with the former astronaut who had been their guide. Before their group left Cheyenne Mountain, she'd been holding his hand. After a bit of checking around, Angelica learned that SSA Sheeran had a reputation for high maintenance and low morals.

Sheeran tossed her long red hair. "It's your first time in the field. Are you having fun yet?"

Apart from being abducted, she was doing okay. "I'm learning."

"I told Spence that he needed to chip you. For once, he listened to me."

To chip me? What was that about? A vague recollection of something about Raquel and Spence teased the edge of her memory, but that wasn't Angelica's focus. She needed to get down to business. "Has there been recent online chatter about NORAD or Cheyenne Mountain?"

"We're not authorized to share."

"What's that supposed to mean?"

Sheeran glanced over her shoulder at the sofa where Spence and the other two agents were fielding objections from Professor Fletcher and his two protégés. With a smug grin, she turned back to Angelica. "I received notification from Quantico that Spence was off this investigation."

So that's the way you want to play this game? Angelica wasn't afraid to dish it out. She squared off, toe-to-toe and wishing she'd been wearing her own high-heeled boots instead of socks. "You weren't contacted by my bosses at NSA."

"Not necessary."

"Are you saying the FBI has jurisdiction over NSA?"

"I don't make those distinctions. All I know is that Spence messed up, and I'm taking over."

Not if I have anything to say about it. "Before I call the director of the NSA—whose number is on my speed dial—let's try to come to an agreement."

"I don't need your cooperation."

"Are you sure about that? You're aware that I was abducted by the perpetrators and escaped. I was with them for hours."

"But you have amnesia."

"I'm remembering more and more all the time—names, dates, passwords, coding numbers."

"You don't scare me."

"Back at you, SSA."

Angelica strolled to the coffee table, picked up the computer and tucked it under her arm. Before she could return to her conversation with Sheeran, the other agent stepped in front of her. The first thing she noticed about him was his shaved head. When he shook her hand, his grasp was reptilian and cold. In spite of his smile, he looked angry.

"Big fan," he said.

She wasn't following. "Okay."

"I'm Special Agent Mike Tapper. We spoke on the phone."

"Right." His name filtered through her memory, and she came up with an answer. He was her direct contact with this field office.

"I appreciate your work in cyber security. That's the future."

"Thanks, Mike."

"I just did a quick sweep of your suite. No bugs."

"I'm looking forward to consulting with you."

"Not so fast." SSA Sheeran stomped toward them. The heels of her boots clunked loudly with each step. "I'll make the decisions about consulting. It's my call."

"Fine." Angelica wrapped both arms around the laptop. "This piece of evidence is in my possession, which makes it part of the NSA investigation."

When Spence joined their little group, he

physically dominated it and towered over everyone else. His rumbling tone of voice betrayed his anger. "Agent Thorne, is SSA Sheeran giving you a hard time?"

"Nothing I can't handle, SA Malone." Angelica gave him a tight-lipped but confident smile. "I was explaining to her that if our two agencies aren't working on a joint basis, sharing information, I'm under no obligation to show her all the delicious clues on this computer."

"You're trying to con me," Sheeran said darkly. She planted her fists on her hips, showing off her hourglass figure. "Why should I believe you?"

Though feeling severely underdressed in her nightgown and robe, Angelica angled a glance toward Spence. "Should I give her a taste?"

"You might as well show her what she's throwing away."

Without looking at the screen, Angelica pulled

up the photo of the murdered man and spun it around so Sheeran could see.

Tapper caught a glimpse and let out a shocked gasp. "Whoa."

Angelica closed the laptop. "And there's more. I'm willing to work together if you are."

"The situation is out of my hands." But her statement was tinged with regret. Maybe Sheeran had finally realized that cooperation was to her benefit. "I'm guessing that you've already copied the content of that computer onto a thumb drive. Am I right?"

Angelica neither confirmed nor denied. "Continue."

"If you give me that thumb drive, I'll tell you the most salient points of recent chatter."

Looking to Spence for confirmation, Angelica asked, "Do you think I should?"

"Do it."

She fished the flash drive out of her bathrobe pocket. "We have a deal."

As soon as she placed the drive onto Sheeran's outstretched palm, the SSA dug into the pocket of her skinny jeans and produced a thumb drive of her own. "This is our recent reading, including stuff from a new clandestine site called Office1116."

That was the same name as the sender on the computer. "We need to compare notes."

"Tomorrow," Sheeran said.

The fact that she'd come prepared with her thumb drive tucked into her pocket told Angelica that the SSA had planned to cooperate from the start. Her objections and hostility reminded her of some kind of hazing ceremony. Angelica couldn't be accepted into the sorority of kickass field agents until she proved herself worthy. "When did you decide to trust me?"

"Maybe I have a soft spot for the tooth fairy." She grinned with half her mouth. "Or maybe I knew we'd work together when I came through the door. You've got a big reputation, Agent Thorne. I'd be a fool not to use you."

Before Sheeran herded her two agents and the three suspects from the room, Angelica stepped close to Fletcher and whispered, "Sorry this happened, Professor."

"Things like this keep life interesting."

"Next time you want to talk to me, just call."

He bobbed his head. "I meant what I said about helping. If you need to use my computers, you have my permission."

She patted his furry cheek and watched as he and the others left. In their absence, the hotel room filled with quiet. Neither she nor Spence moved. They stood on opposite sides of the sofa as frozen as her memories.

A hazy recollection began to form in the back of her mind. Not too long ago, they'd talked about the fiery red-haired agent.

"What's the date?" Angelica asked.

"Since it's after midnight, it's November four-teenth."

"When did you first hear from Sheeran?"

"She contacted my supervisor," he said. "About three weeks ago, she reported unusual cyber activity that indicated a possible hack into NORAD."

Her memory became more distinct. She spun around and faced him. His jeans and T-shirt fit so well that they might have been designed especially for him. He had the kind of body that made any outfit—from a tuxedo to sweat-pants—look good. He was a catch. She knew it and so did a lot of other women, including Sheeran.

"She wanted you for the investigation," Angelica said. "She asked for you."

His jaw tensed. "We've had this conversation before."

"I forgot."

"Let's hear it for amnesia!" He strode across

the room and gathered her into an embrace. "Finally, I catch a break."

"Hold on." Though leaning her head against his shoulder felt incredibly comfortable, she reared back and stared up at him. "I need to remember. Amnesia is the enemy."

"But there are a hundred things more important for you to recall than an old argument."

He kissed her forehead and went into the bedroom where he grabbed the room service cart and wheeled it back into the central room of the suite to the table. As he arranged his place setting, he said, "I've got a couple of memory techniques I want to use with you."

He gave a brief explanation of relaxation and meditation that she barely listened to. Her attention was still fixated on Sheeran. The date November sixteenth rose up in her mind. One-one-one-six was, for some reason, important. When Spence picked up the champagne and prepared to pop the cork, she wondered if drinking was such a good idea when they should be concentrating.

"Don't worry," he said, reading her mind. "This is nonalcoholic. I wouldn't give you booze when we're not sure what kind of drugs are in your system."

"Thoughtful." Actually, it was doubly thoughtful. First, he was being considerate about her physical condition. Second, he'd remembered that champagne was her favorite.

The cork exploded from the bottle. A few drops spilled before Spence captured the fizzy liquid in a long-stemmed glass from room service. He handed it to her before pouring one of his own. Gazing at her over the rim, he proposed a toast. "Here's to my sweet angel who's a lot tougher than she looks."

She took a sip. The bubbles tickled her nose. "Do I look fragile? I mean, if it came to a show-down between me and Sheeran, do you think I could take her down?"

"You just did," he said as he sat at the table. "I don't want to talk about her anymore."

She sat beside him at the table, sipping the phony champagne that tasted as good as the real stuff. Though not hungry, she picked bits of lettuce and soggy croutons from the salad. The flash drive Sheeran had given her weighed heavily in the pocket of her robe. She couldn't wait to plug it in. The Office1116 reference gave her hope that there was other useful evidence.

"What if it's a date," she said.

He chewed slowly and swallowed. "You're talking about the one-one-one-six. I thought of that when I first saw the email name. One of my accounts is Spence421."

"No way." How did she ever get hooked up with this guy who was so unsavvy about computers? "You used your first name and your birthday?"

"Not very original."

"No, you Luddite, not very clever at all."

"If the date is eleven-sixteen, we're talking about two days from right now. A mere forty-eight hours."

With very little time to decipher the threat and stop it, she and Spence needed to be smart and lucky. If they failed, the result might be nuclear catastrophe.

Chapter Eleven

"This is never going to work," Angelica said as she stormed into the bedroom of their hotel suite.

Though Spence would have preferred to have her stretched out in bed and naked, he directed her to a contemporary-style chaise longue. "It's important for you to remember. You were inside NORAD."

"I've gotten a lot of my memory back."

"Sit on the chaise and get comfortable. If you need pillows or an extra blanket, tell me."

"We're wasting time. We could be going over the data on the FBI flash drive."

"Later." If any of the information Sheeran had compiled included vital or actionable evidence, he was damn sure she wouldn't wait around for them to discover it. How had he ever dated that woman? She insisted on being the boss, which was probably why they never got seriously intimate.

"I hate this," she muttered.

"I'm aware."

"Don't take it personally. It's not you. It's me, my problem." She stood at the end of the chaise with her arms folded around her middle in a classic posture of resistance. "I'm not a good candidate for hypnosis. Other people have tried...and failed. It's just not my thing."

"Sit," he said.

"Ordering me around won't help." But she plunked down on the edge of the chaise.

Stiff as a stick, her rigid spine and clenched jaw were a textbook definition of *tense*. His job was to get her to relax enough to open her mind and let the memories flow. "You don't look comfortable."

"I'm just fine."

He told himself that he, too, was just fine. Not true. Spence suffered from his own distractions. Three paces to his left was a king-size bed with the covers already pulled down and the smooth white sheets waiting for them. A powerful urge tore through him as he imagined making an imprint on those sheets. He cherished those moments when his body pressed down on her and she arched her back and fused with him. They became one.

How could she sit there, so prim and proper, when all he wanted was to shred her clothes and claim her sweet mouth with kisses? It had only been five days since they were in bed together. Had the amnesia made her forget how good it was? Even when they argued, their sexual chemistry surpassed anything he'd experienced before.

In a hoarse voice, he said, "Let's get this over with."

"What do you want me to do?"

"Loosen up, scoot back on the chaise. Open up your arms."

Giving her the time and space to cooperate, he dimmed the lights in the bedroom and selected a classical playlist on his computer. He'd thought far enough ahead to order a candle from room service when they brought the meal. He lit the votive and placed it on the small table beside the chaise.

Still, she hadn't relaxed. Her arms thrust straight down at her side, her knees rubbed together and she stared straight ahead.

Fighting his natural arousal, he took action. As gently as possible, he bent her elbows. When he rested his hands on either side of her slim waist, he asked, "Does this hurt? I don't want to press against your bruise."

"You aren't touching it," she said. "But what are you doing?"

"Forcing you to relax."

"Oxymoron."

"I don't care."

He lifted her and adjusted her position so that her back rested against the chaise. After straightening her nightgown and robe, he stretched her legs straight out in front. Now at least she didn't look like an ice sculpture.

Touching her was having a predictable effect on him. The blood surged like lava through his veins. The opposite of Angelica, he was so damn hot that he was sweating under his T-shirt.

He pulled up a smaller chair and sat beside her. "Close your eyes."

"Is this when you work your magic and hypnotize me?"

"If I had to call this exercise anything, I'd say guided meditation."

"Well, now you sound like a guru." She smirked. "I'd rather have you be a magician, waving a shiny object back and forth in front of my face and telling me that I'm getting sleepy, sleepy, sleepy."

He'd about had it with her attitude. "We don't have to do this. To tell the truth, I'd rather not."

"What would you rather do?"

"I'd rather kiss you. Would rather tear off your clothes and lick every inch of your body."

Her eyes narrowed to emerald slits. "I remember what that's like."

"So do I."

"Sex was one of my first real memories to return," she said. "At the pastor's house, I remembered making love after we saw *Camelot*."

In a desperate effort, he clutched the tattered shreds of his willpower, keeping his bottom in the chair instead of diving on top of her. More to himself than to her, he said, "This is my job."

"Mine, too. I'm your partner."

"We're a team, and I need for you to remember. You spent hours with the bad guys, and there must have been something you saw or heard. The stuff locked up inside your pretty little head is some of our best evidence."

"Okay, I'll try."

A shudder rocked her shoulders as she reined herself into control. He felt her putting distance between them. Though he'd said that was what he wanted, Spence nearly wept when she looked away from him. "Angelica, are you okay?"

"What do I have to do?"

Jumping into peaceful meditation probably wouldn't work until they had both settled down. "We should talk for a while, get back on track."

"There's only one thing on my mind," she said. "All those really juicy, really good memories you've given me."

He deserved a medal for staying on course. "You mentioned not being a good subject. Have you been hypnotized before?"

"Once," she said. "On a family vacation when I was sixteen, we went to a magic show. We had great seats near the front, and when the magician asked for volunteers, my sister raised her hand. He took both of us. The identical twin thing appeals to a lot of people."

"What was the magician's name?"

"The act was a man and woman, Nightshade and Belladonna. Actually, they were pretty good at mind reading, which is only a matter of codes and numbers."

"The hypnosis," he said, pulling her back from a digression.

"He did his relax-and-sleep thing, and my sister went right under. Not me. He tried again. I was still wide-awake."

"A performer's nightmare."

"Mr. Nightshade whispered in my ear that if I played along, he'd give me fifty bucks after the show." She shrugged. "I faked it. Squawked like a chicken and did a hula dance. My sister upstaged me by acting out a death scene for a chicken. She loves an audience."

"Did he pay you?"

"Yeah, and he gave me some free advice. He told me that people who can't get hypnotized have trust issues."

Spence had noticed that tendency in her. Others might consider her natural mistrust to be a character flaw, but he appreciated her caution. He, too, had been burned enough times to be initially suspicious. "Was Nightshade right?"

"Probably," she said with a shrug. "A shrink told me the same thing after several hours of therapy and a boatload of cash."

Never before had she mentioned going to a shrink. He wanted to hear more but not right now. "Let's get started."

"Can I ask a question first?"

"Shoot."

"Why did the FBI wait so long to start investigating? Evidence of hacking showed up three weeks ago, which was when Sheeran reported a problem. Nothing was done."

"The data passed from desk to desk and there were meetings, but nobody took it seriously. That's why they sent the two of us—a small reconnaissance team to poke around." He'd already had this conversation with her, but hesitated to point it out. "Is any of this ringing a bell?"

"I just can't understand. We're talking about nuclear missiles, bombs that can devastate an entire city. Why wouldn't they do something?"

"Sit back and get ready for a history lesson."

"I already know all about NORAD."

"So you know that technology is a hell of a lot different now than when the complex was first built in the late 1950s."

"I've seen photographs of the early days."

"Those computers were the size of SUVs, even bigger. They took up whole rooms."

"It was a different world," she said. "Somebody like me wouldn't have fit in very well."

"NORAD headquarters was where they kept the most sophisticated electronic equipment. There's still a lot of top secret data and monitoring that goes on there, and Cheyenne Mountain is considered the best place to resist an attack by electromagnetic pulse. But the computers inside the granite mountain are no longer impregnable. Hackers have found a way."

"Even when they get in, there are enough security redundancies to stop tampering or launches." A smile touched her lips. "You've told me this before."

Her memory gave reason for hope. More might slip through the veil of amnesia. "You remember."

"Your voice," she said, "when you said words like *electromagnetic pulse*, *EMP* and *impregnable*. I like the way your mouth moved while you spoke."

He needed to start the relaxing techniques before they got too far into watching each other's mouth. "Close your eyes."

In a low, slow tone, he instructed her to relax her feet and toes, then her legs, then her fingers and so on. He kept his own eyes closed to avoid checking out each delicious body part. If he allowed himself to get aroused, she'd hear the suppressed excitement in his voice and get distracted. *Not yet.* He needed to concentrate on the missing hours when she'd been abducted.

When her breathing reflected what he hoped was an inner serenity, he said, "Open your eyes. Focus on the flame of the candle."

Through half-lidded eyes, she followed his instructions. "Just so you know," she said, "I'm not asleep."

"It's okay. This isn't a magic show." He thought of Nightshade dealing with bright-eyed, brave, energetic Angelica. "Now I want you to slowly count backward from five."

"Five…four…three…" She completed the sequence.

"Keep watching the candle," he said. "Last night, we went to your parents' house in separate cars."

"Because you needed to stop off at FBI headquarters later, and I wanted to leave early to see Mom and Dad."

They never should have split up. Spence had been too casual, treating this assignment more like a vacation than a mission. She was right. They were dealing with nukes. He should have taken their actions more seriously. "Tell me about the weather while you were driving."

"It was a blue sky day until the sun dipped behind the Sangre de Cristo mountain range and the horizon turned to yellow and pink and orange. I was happy because this was my first field assignment…"

He'd known how proud she was to be out from behind her desk. Didn't quite understand the thrill, but he'd seen her excitement when she slipped her Glock into a holster under her blazer rather than carrying it in her purse.

She continued, "And I was eager to have my parents meet you. As soon as I walked in the door, Dad let me know he didn't like the idea of me being involved with another agent."

He'd sensed hostility from the general, who had gone to the trouble of looking him up on the internet. Spence's college degrees from second-rate institutions, paid for with football scholarships, made him proud. He'd achieved more than he'd ever expected. But her father pointed out that he wasn't exactly the product of an Ivy League education, wasn't good enough for his daughter.

This was a discussion for later. He moved her through the night. "When we left, I went first so I could check in with SSA Sheeran. You were going to follow."

"I stayed a bit longer than I planned to," she

admitted. "Dad wanted to know why we weren't engaged."

Spence cursed himself. He should have given her that diamond he'd been carrying around for weeks. Oh, yeah, they definitely needed to talk when this was over. "And then you drove back to the hotel."

"In the parking lot…" Her sentence trailed off. Though she continued to stare at the candle, she blinked. "It happened almost exactly as I surmised. I was hit by a stun gun, then I was shoved into the trunk of a car and drugged."

She cringed, probably recalling the pain as she touched her hip where she had the bruise.

"In the trunk," he prompted, "could you see anything?"

"Too dark. And I was mostly unconscious. It was stinky, though. Exhaust fumes. And then… I woke up, sitting on a wood chair. My head jerked back."

"And you could see."

"I had on a black hood, but I could look out of the bottom. I had on a sweatshirt. My wrists were duct taped to the arms of the chair."

Her voice had dropped to a whisper as though fearful that someone might overhear. She darted a glance to the right and to the left. Her arms bent at the elbow, mimicking the position she'd described.

Her reaction was even better than he'd hoped. She appeared to be reliving the memory. He needed to choose his words carefully, to keep her in that time and place.

Gently, he asked, "Were you alone?"

"People were talking." Her head tilted back and she looked up. "The overhead lights were so bright that I could see them through the weave in the hood."

He offered a suggestion. "And they were still talking."

"Yes, and I tried to listen. They talked about a

Five men? That m
met up with Trevor
scribe the accent."

"He kept talking
was Texan. I wish I
eyebrows pulled do
descriptions. A fielc
member details."

"You're doing fin

"They set a comp
me to input the hacl
ured out. That was
ing they could do v
secrets."

"Did they try?"

"They were all tal
typing in codes for
rejected. But one ol
stopped me. I mad
She blinked several
off, but I recognize

boss, someone who was older than them. They didn't mention names."

While he'd waited for her at the hotel, he'd gotten a text from her cell phone saying that she was spending the night at her parents' house because she and her mom had a lot to talk about.

Though he hadn't liked her plan, he decided to be understanding. The next morning, he had another text, telling him that she had an opportunity to go inside Cheyenne Mountain Complex with minimal supervision. A friend of her dad arranged it, and she wanted to take advantage.

When he tried to call her back, he was steamed, and she didn't answer. His instincts sensed something was wrong. He tried using the GPS tracking device he'd implanted in her arm but couldn't get a signal. If she'd been inside the mountain, that made sense. His GPS wouldn't work under tons of granite.

The next few hours crawled past. He vacillated between telling himself there was noth-

ing to worry ab
Without alerting
kidnapping, he t
Angelica hadn't
headquarters. N
in Cheyenne Co
in the hotel park

True panic set
started beeping,
into the mountai

He returned to
off the hood, yo

"Nothing spec
with cubicles an
ilar to the setup

"But not Peter

"I couldn't see
wore ski masks
rubber gloves,
bright like Magl
had an accent."

And he paid for his clumsiness with his life. "Did you say his name?"

"No."

"What did he do?"

"He yelled. After that, I don't remember much."

Her bravery touched him. The longer this exercise dragged on, the less he cared about the mission and the more he worried about her. Disregarding subtlety and guiding her along the path to remembrance, he took her hand.

"Did they hurt you?"

"I don't think so." She squeezed his fingers. Her touch was warm. "They asked if I wanted water or food. For a while, I was fastened to the arms of a chair but they used duct tape over the sweatshirt, nothing painful. On the other hand, they drugged me and took my memory."

"This is enough for tonight," he said. "I'm going to count backward from five and clap my hands."

"Don't bother," she said. "I'm not in a trance."

"Humor me. Five...four...three..."

"I overheard them say something about how it only takes one to show we mean business. Only one, one strike and we get top dollar for the other six."

He stopped counting. "A strike."

"And I know where they're going to attack."

Chapter Twelve

"Dallas," she said.

During the relaxation exercise, Angelica hadn't been hypnotized. Spence's voice soothed her, and he seemed to know all the right questions to prod her memory, but she hadn't succumbed to any kind of hocus-pocus spell. Conscious and aware of what she was saying, she'd been able to go deep and mine the memories from hidden corners of her brain. And she'd hit gold.

"It worked," Spence said.

"In a way," she conceded. "I remembered a bit more."

"You really hate to admit that I might be right."

He swooped, lifted her from the chaise and carried her to the bed. His caveman habit of picking her up was irritating but also sexy. In a primitive part of her psyche, she enjoyed his ability to dominate her with his greater size and strength. Never would she admit to such an old-fashioned attitude, but there it was.

His mesmerizing blue eyes raked over her face. When he was close like this, she didn't care about whether or not she could trust him or her dad's disapproval or the lack of an engagement proposal. He lay beside her. Her everything, he was all she wanted. She grabbed the front of his T-shirt and pulled him close.

"Dallas," he said. "I knew you had evidence buried in your subconscious. Our hacking threat just got specific."

With a groan, she ripped her gaze away from his handsome face, flopped back against the pillows and stared at the ceiling. "I suppose we have to deal with this."

"I need to get reassigned to the case."

Her lust would have to be put on hold. She was a field agent and needed to direct all her energy into their mission. Didn't seem fair but she'd have to wait to make love—until after they saved the world.

"We should hurry," she said. They'd already talked about the possibility of the Office1116 username in the emails pertaining to a date: eleven-sixteen. "The strike might be scheduled for the sixteenth, which is two days from today."

He tore open the sash on her robe and ripped the terry cloth open. Underneath, she still wore her blue-and-gray-striped nightgown, but that fabric was thin and clingy. When he lowered himself on top of her, she felt every hard ridge of his six-pack abs. His demanding kiss stole her breath away.

"I'll be back." He bolted across the room and grabbed his cell phone.

Though still dazed by their intense moment of contact, she managed to speak. "Wait! It's too late to call anybody on the East Coast."

"Protocol goes out the window when it comes to nukes."

With his cell phone at his ear, he left her alone on the king-size bed. Field agent protocol suggested that she make a few calls of her own. But she wasn't anxious to inform her supervisor that she'd been abducted, given amnesia and discovered a murder victim.

She threw off the covers and retrieved her personal laptop from her luggage. This machine wasn't powerful enough or well protected enough to dive into the dark web where she could research the codes from the emails: Y75110 and C4ICBM. From what she'd overheard while being held by the bad guys, she figured that something would be offered for sale, probably at a limited auction, probably after the strike on Dallas proved they had the capability to launch.

In the pocket of her robe, she found the FBI flash drive she'd gotten from Sheeran. An image of the red-haired SSA wearing a skintight, strapless gown tickled another memory. A photograph, where had she seen it? Angelica shoved those thoughts aside; she wasn't ready to go deep again.

Sprawled across the bed on her belly with the computer open in front of her, she plugged in the flash drive. The data displayed in a pattern of icons and files that she recognized as being similar to those used by Heller and his merry crew at Peterson AFB.

There was an array of maps, ranging from satellite photos to hand-drawn cartography. The area displayed was mostly Western United States and Canada, which made sense. NORAD was a joint operation between the two nations, designed to cover this part of the world with a protective net. Some of the markings on the maps indicated the facilities and silos where the weapons were kept.

Growing up near NORAD, she had a clearer understanding than most of the size and scope of this decades-old program. Numbers varied, depending on the source, but there were probably over five thousand active nuclear warheads and hundreds of launch missiles to send them on their way. Some had been decommissioned. Others updated.

A shudder went through her. She hated to imagine that someone had gotten control of these missiles and was able to launch at will. One strike could destroy Dallas, and the voices she'd overheard said there were six more. Seven missiles? No matter how far-fetched, that threat was enough to restart the Cold War.

In other files, there were memos from Peterson AFB, projections and lists of supplies.

There were also transcripts of conversations regarding the NORAD hack, including a talk she'd had with Professor Fletcher. Seeing her words transcribed and documented was a little bit creepy. More worrisome was the fact that the FBI recorded a call with the professor. Were they monitoring him or keeping track of calls made on his phone? Their conversation never mentioned NORAD; they'd been discussing obscure cryptography software.

She homed in on the file labeled Office1116. Sources for the information were untraceable but she did learn a few interesting things. Lex Heller claimed to be her close friend, and he suspected her of holding out on information. He used the phrase "on account of the old man" a couple of times. As soon as she read the words, she heard them in her memory. References to the "old man." What did her father have to do with any of this?

The "old man" could also be the professor.

She hated that Office1116 had anything at all to say about her and people she knew and loved. Professor Fletch wasn't a traitor and would never do anything to harm anyone else. Still, she reminded herself, the photo of the murder had been delivered to his doorstep.

Office1116 mentioned the three cities—Dallas, Seattle and Seoul—several times. There were mileage charts indicating how far these cities were from Colorado Springs and from other unnamed locations. She had the pieces to the puzzle but didn't know how it all fit together.

Sometimes, the solution to a problem required distance, similar to those artworks that looked like a bunch of dots when you were close and coalesced into recognizable forms when you stepped back. If she could print out the maps and equations, she might see the connections. Those types of graphics required different software than she had on her laptop.

She thought of Professor Fletch. He had exactly the type of computer she needed. Twice, he'd offered the use of his equipment, which she hoped was nothing more than goodwill on his part. She didn't want to think he was somehow involved and trying to send her a message.

She got out of bed, rotated her shoulders, stretched her arms and yawned. Considering all that she'd put her body through in the past few days, she wasn't feeling too much discomfort. Slowly, she paced across the carpet. The large bruise on her side was tender. Other than that, her aches and pains were minimal.

Through the half-opened door, she overheard her name.

Talking into his phone, Spence said, "Agent Thorne has the expertise required for the job."

She appreciated his vote of confidence. Too bad she didn't share his enthusiasm for her ability to solve a complex problem.

"If we need help, we can use the local resources," Spence said. "This close to NORAD, you can't swing a cat without hitting a computer nerd."

When he ended the call, she slipped through the door and went to him. Her hands crept under his T-shirt and glided up his muscular torso and chest. "Are we on the case?"

"With the full support of Quantico," he said, raising his arms and pulling the shirt off over his head.

The light fur on his bare chest enticed her. She stroked with her palms while her fingers traced a path. The man was, as she had noticed so many times before, gorgeous.

"Did you hear what I said?" he asked. "I didn't mean to call you a nerd."

"I'm proudly nerd-like." Touching him made her pulse accelerate. Still, she tried to sound nonchalant. "But your metaphor should have been about a mouse, like a computer mouse.

Don't say you can't swing a cat. You can't swing a mouse."

He placed his index finger across her lips. "No more talk."

She couldn't have agreed more. This time, she didn't allow herself to be slung over his shoulder like a piece of meat. Moving fast, she latched on to his hand and tugged him across the front room into the bedroom. Once there, she halted and they collapsed onto the bed wrapped in each other's arms.

Her need had never been greater. From the first moment she saw him, she had remembered that they were good in bed. Images of that past history replayed in her mind. Usually, they engaged in a reasonable amount of foreplay, gradually building to a climax.

Tonight was different.

Instead of a slow climb, she shot to the edge of the highest cliff. With her toes curled over the ledge, she stared into a thrilling abyss, ready to leap. Her breath came in ragged gasps. She arched her back, threw back her head and roared a feral cry of desperation and desire.

He lay on top of her and held her face in both of his huge hands, forcing her to meet his gaze.

"My sweet angel," he whispered. "I thought I'd lost you."

"No such luck."

"This isn't a joke." He kept her pinned. Though she bucked against him, he had her completely under his control. "If anything bad happened to you, I'd demand my vengeance."

"That's enough, Spence. I thought we were done talking."

"Whatever you want, angel."

He kissed her lightly. Too gentle, she wanted more. "Harder."

"Your lip is bleeding."

With the tip of her tongue, she tasted the blood. Her split lip from the escape through the snow hadn't altogether healed, not that she felt the pain. "It doesn't hurt."

"I'll find somewhere else to kiss."

He grabbed fistfuls of striped fabric and yanked her nightgown up and over her head. Stretched out on the sheets below him, she was naked, reveling in the subtle whisper of air across her skin.

His hands cupped her breasts, and his thumbs flicked the tight, rose-colored tips. When he ducked his head and suckled, an ever-expanding ripple of pleasure consumed her. Again, she cried out. Frantic and near climax, she wanted him inside her.

With her legs still spread, she sat up. Her fingers grappled with the waistband of his sweatpants. Through the fabric, she felt his thick, hard shaft.

He set her hands aside, rose from the bed and stripped. *Gorgeous!* Driven by uncontrollable forces, she wrestled her arms around him and dragged him onto the sheets, positioning herself to climb all over his muscular body. Her legs splayed across his lower abdomen, and she dragged herself lower until his erection eased between her thighs. At last, she joined herself with him. He filled her completely.

For a long moment, she didn't make a move. Nor did he. Their breathing synchronized. Their hearts beat as one.

Inside her, he twitched. That small movement was exciting, excruciating. *More, she wanted more.* Her muscles tensed as she gripped him.

"So sweet," he whispered as his arms encircled her.

When he flipped her onto her back and rose up above her, she knew foreplay was most definitely over. Starting fast, he plowed her thoroughly, and then he pulled out, slowly, almost to the tip, before plunging deeper. An orgasm rocked her from the inside out.

He didn't stop. While she was exploding beneath him, he kept going, pushing her to even greater heights. Finally, when she thought she couldn't take it anymore, he gave one final thrust. They finished together.

While her muscles fluttered and goose bumps marched up and down her bare thighs, her mind filled with visions of fireworks and starry nights. She wasn't sure how much she remembered, but this had to be the best sex ever.

Chapter Thirteen

Early that morning, they got on the road and headed up to the mountains. Spence almost kept driving when he recognized the shiny red pickup truck parked outside Pastor Clarence's cabin. "I don't suppose it's a coincidence that your dad is here."

"Afraid not," she said. "I called him this morning to tell him I couldn't go out to lunch, and I might have mentioned a visit to the pastor and Trudy."

Neither of those lovely people were the real reason Spence had returned to the cabin. Special Agent Trevor MacArthur was staying here with his aunt and uncle while his supervisors in Quantico figured out the next direction for his undercover work. While Trevor was here, Spence wanted him to show them the place where he and his three cronies met with Heller after he picked up Angelica. The location might trigger more memories from her.

So far, their best clues had come from the bits she recalled when she was being held captive, namely "a strike on Dallas in two days." When he'd warned his supervisors at Quantico, they set a lot of other investigative trails into motion. He and Angelica were to continue with what they'd started, and they'd be working alone unless they requested assistance.

SSA Sheeran and the other local agents could be used for backup and in specific situations. When Spence had talked to her on the phone this morning and informed her that her involvement wasn't needed, Sheeran accused him of not trusting her. And she was correct; he didn't trust anybody. The way he figured, the strike had to be an inside job. Personnel at Peterson AFB were compromised. The murder of Lex Heller was proof of that. The FBI field office was too close to the problem.

He parked on the road behind her father's truck. In the daylight with a blue sky overhead, the snow-covered cabin and rustic church were charming. The pastor and Trudy had carved out a pleasant life for themselves, except for her chronic illness.

Angelica let herself out of the SUV before he could come around to open her door. "It's as pretty as a postcard and a long way off the beaten path, but you'd never find Pastor Clarence's church unless you were looking for it."

"Your dad knew where it was."

"He knows everything," she said. "He might be retired, but he tries to run his mountain community the way he ran his command, with his sticky fingers in every pie."

Though she wasn't praising her father, Spence could see how much she loved the general. When she spoke of him, her eyes brightened and she couldn't help smiling.

Following her up the shoveled path to the front porch, Spence braced himself for a dose of her father's hostility. At their first meeting, the general had been mildly unpleasant, but now he knew his daughter was involved in a dangerous investigation. Spence figured he'd be fortunate to escape with all his body parts still attached.

He placed his hand possessively on her shoulder. Yesterday, she would have shrugged him off and called him unprofessional. Today, she stepped into a closer embrace and gazed up with warm, sexy eyes that set off a chain reaction inside his gut. His hand slid down her back and up under her parka to cup her jean-clad bottom. He'd always been attracted to her, but not like this. After last night, he was obsessed. Their lovemaking had been more than satisfying.

General Peter Thorne flung open the door to confront them. Though he wore a red-and-gray plaid sweater, his posture was appropriate for a full-dress uniform. He was a dignified man, a figure of authority. His hair was thinning and pure white, but he made up for that lack of hair with bushy black eyebrows. He barely glanced at Spence, reserving all his attention for his daughter, who greeted him with a hug and a kiss on the cheek.

Before he had a chance to read her the riot act, she said, "Don't try to change my mind. This is my job. I want you to respect that."

"You stumbled over a dead body," he said. "It's too damn dangerous."

"My job," she repeated. "My decision."

Her statement was not unexpected, and her dad was ready with a different solution. "At least let me assign a couple of bodyguards to follow you around."

"Don't need them," she said as she tapped Spence on the chest. "I've got him."

Trudy bustled up to join them. "Spence can handle that job. I'll tell you, General Thorne, this young man is very brave. He didn't back down a single inch when Angelica came after him with her violin bow."

Her dad hoisted his brows. "Dear woman, what are you talking about?"

"Let's chat over tea and cookies." She directed them to the very long table where she had arranged two platefuls of different cookies, orange juice and a tea service.

Angelica embraced Trudy and the pastor before moving on to the munchies. Spence didn't move fast enough to follow. Her dad steered him into a detour.

"You know I'm right," the general said in a low growl. "She shouldn't be doing this."

"Here's what I know." Spence matched his tone with a gravelly whisper of his own. "Angelica is smart, competent and trained as a field agent. She can find the answers. In so doing, she'll save countless lives."

"At what personal cost? I don't want her in danger."

"A few days ago, I slipped up." Spence didn't mention that the reason for Angelica being in danger was her desire to stay behind and make things right with her father. "I promise you, it won't happen again."

"If you fail—"

"If I can't keep her safe, I'll be dead." He'd gladly sacrifice himself for her, but that wasn't his preferred course of action. "And my funeral plan doesn't take effect for another sixty years."

He excused himself and found Pastor Clarence, who thanked him for getting the general to visit. The pastor's plans for Peter Thorne included a trip to a soup kitchen in Colorado

Springs for a Thanksgiving feast and using his powerful basso to sing in Trudy's choir.

Spence interrupted, "Where's Trevor?"

"He's in the garage, warming up my car. He didn't think it'd be wise to meet up with Angelica's dad. When you leave, pull into the church parking lot and wait for a minute. He'll drive past and honk, and then you follow him."

Spence could tell that the pastor enjoyed playing spy. "Should I honk back?"

"Probably not," he said. "We don't want to make too much noise. The general will catch on."

"How can I be sure it's Trevor?"

The pastor scratched his head. "I never thought of that."

"We'll take our chances."

He signaled to Angelica, and she quickly wrapped up with her dad and gave Trudy a pair of acoustic, sound-canceling headphones to listen to her music.

"I thought you might like these," Angelica said. "I had them in my luggage, and I have another pair back home in Virginia."

"Thank you, dear." Trudy popped the dark purple headphones over her gray hair and beamed a smile. "Do I look like a hip grandma?"

Angelica nodded. "The hippest."

After another few moments, they were out the door and into the SUV. Following instructions, Spence drove into the church parking lot, which had been cleared by a snowplow. He barely had time to turn the SUV around before he heard a car horn and saw a blue Volvo sedan, probably ten years old and equipped with all-wheel drive. With a crank of the wheel, he exited onto the road and fell in line behind Trevor.

"I've been thinking," she said, "how remarkable it was that you found me. Trevor never mentioned that he contacted you with the location of the van."

"He didn't." Spence had a bad feeling about where her line of reasoning might be leading.

"I could have been anywhere."

With a sense of impending trouble, he tried to divert her thinking. "The important thing is that I found you."

Undeterred, she continued, "There isn't much surveillance in the mountains, so I doubt you spotted the van on a camera feed. Even if you did, you wouldn't know I was inside unless Lex Heller passed on that information. But he didn't. What was it that pointed you in the right direction and led you to me?"

He said nothing. There were no words to make this right. The truth was indefensible.

"Aha!" she said. "Last night SSA Sheeran mentioned something about a chip. Would you care to explain?"

"Not really."

"Let me fill in the blank," she said. "You im-

planted a chip to enable GPS tracking in me…
without my permission."

"For your protection."

"Before we left Quantico, you asked me if I
minded having a chip implanted, and I said that
I didn't want one. I refused. You did it, anyway.
You chipped me like an implanted ID on a dog.
Or a LoJack system on a car."

Her laser-edged glare seared off chunks of his
flesh. He understood her outrage, but he wasn't
going to apologize. The chip had worked exactly the way it was intended. The reason he'd
been able to locate her in the sprawling mountain landscape was the tiny blip on a computer
screen that marked her whereabouts.

"Here's what hurts," she said. "You never
would have put in the chip if you trusted me.
You figured I'd mess up, and you'd have to rescue me."

"I didn't see it that way."

"Answer me this," she challenged, "have you

chipped any of your other partners? Or have you worn a GPS chip of your own?"

He could have gone through a complicated rationalization about how undercover agents can't have any implanted devices, but that didn't excuse him. All the justification in the world couldn't erase her logical conclusion that he didn't trust her.

Spence concentrated on the road. Trevor was leading them down from the secluded mountain area populated by a few cabins and many acres of National Forest. At the lower elevation, the packed snow on the road had melted in patches.

"I should have trusted you," he said.

"A tracking chip is something my father would do."

"I'm not like him." That was a comparison he could do without. "I wanted to keep you safe."

"You can't swaddle me in Bubble Wrap."

He didn't like to admit when he was wrong,

but he wouldn't cling to a mistake. He hadn't given her enough credit, hadn't trusted her. "I'm sorry."

"Accepted."

He glanced at her stony profile. She'd forgiven him, but he was damn sure this was going to be one of those relationship issues she'd want to discuss. They'd disagreed about trust before. Angelica felt that trust came as an inseparable part of the love package, along with caring, respecting and sharing. On the other hand, he took a more pragmatic approach. Trust wasn't given but earned. If she wanted him to trust her as a field agent, she needed to step up her game.

At a crossroads, the Volvo turned into a parking lot for a market, café, gas station and small motel. Spence followed in the SUV. The name of the motel appeared to be Hog Heaven and the sign was decorated with the neon outline of a pig with a curly tail. On the back side of the motel, Trevor parked, got out of the car and came toward them. He slapped Spence on the back and gave Angelica a hug.

Looking her over, he said, "Last time we met, you'd barely pulled yourself together. You clean up nice."

"So do you."

"Trudy's been stuffing me from morning to night." He gestured in the general direction of an abandoned porta potty that sat on one end of the building to a ramshackle shed on the other. "This is where we picked you up from Heller."

The asphalt parking lot stretched to the edge of a forested hillside. Dirty snow piled up in the shadow of the Dumpster. There was no one else in sight.

Spence shrugged. "Not exactly the type of place you'd want to store in your memory."

"There's something familiar. I'm not sure what it is." She hiked to the end of the parking lot and went past the porta potty, giving it a wide berth.

Spence turned to Trevor and asked, "Have you ever worn a GPS tracking implant?"

"Hell, no. I try to stay off the grid."

Spence felt the same way when he was working alone. "Suppose you had a partner."

"No chips," Trevor said. "I'd have to trust my partner to stay in touch."

And there was that word again. *Trust.* Spence shook his head and refocused on the task at hand. "When you and the three goons picked Angelica up, was she conscious?"

"Barely," he said. "Without letting the other idiots know, I took her vitals. Her breathing and pulse were regular. Her hands were cold."

He hated hearing about what she went through, even though she'd assured him that she wasn't badly mistreated. And he swore that he wouldn't leave her unguarded for the rest of the time they were in Colorado.

She came back around the building. "I remember the Hog Heaven sign but not from when Heller brought me here. This place is the turnoff that leads to Professor Fletcher's cabin."

The location was handy because they had plans to go to the cabin where the professor kept some unusual computers. But Spence didn't like having her old mentor connected in any way to the strike on Dallas. Good old Fletch made a good suspect because he knew computers, the photograph of the murdered Lex Heller had been delivered to his doorstep and Angelica had remembered references to "the old man," a description that suited the bearded professor.

After he thanked Trevor for his help, Spence drove around front and parked. Angelica had accepted his apology, but he felt the need for bonding and making things right between them. He arranged papers in a folder and handed it to her. "Get ready for some boring fieldwork."

"Doing what?"

"Questioning possible witnesses," he said. "We need to talk to the people in the motel, café and market. They might have noticed an important detail."

In the folder were ID photos of Lex Heller, Bo Lambert, Howie Dunne and the professor. Also, a photo of the van used to transport her. When Angelica paged through the assortment, she chuckled. "This is so old-school. I could call these pictures up on my computer tablet."

"Feel free," he said. "Is there anybody else you suspect? There are probably mug shots of the three thugs who were with Trevor. I don't like SA Ramirez. Add him to the lineup."

"And SSA Raquel Sheeran," she said as she flipped through identification programs. "She's got some of that evil dominatrix thing going on."

"Good call." He had no problem thinking of Sheeran as a woman in leather with a whip. "Add her and no more than two others."

"Because we don't want to overwhelm the witnesses," she said. Her mood improved significantly as she set up her array of photos and computer images. "Can I ask the questions?"

"Knock yourself out."

He followed her into the motel office, a worn-out room with a counter, a dead ficus and a sign-in book. None of the names in the book were their suspects, but he took a photo with his phone for possible evidentiary use.

She did all the talking, and she was good at it, hitting exactly the right note between authority and friendliness. Her natural poise kept these suspects on their toes as they went from the motel to the bar to the market. Spence was impressed that none of the men hit on her.

The kid with a military buzz cut who sat behind the cash register in the market identified the professor as someone who lived around here and sometimes came in to buy stuff. He got excited about Sheeran, not that he recognized her, but he sure did like those redheads.

Back in the SUV, they compared notes. None

of these men had seen or heard anything un-usual. Angelica had done a good job with the in-terviews, and he'd told her so. When he reached across the console and patted her shoulder, she shrugged him away. Now what had he done wrong? Dreading the answer, he asked, "Do we have a problem?"

"Looking at the photo of Raquel Sheeran, I remembered another picture." Her tone was frosty. "She's wearing a strapless formal gown covered with sequins. A man in a tuxedo stands beside her. That man is you."

Chapter Fourteen

"I'm not a jealous woman," Angelica said as she plugged Professor Fletcher's mountain address into the SUV's GPS. "Follow these directions. We'll be there in twenty minutes."

"We already talked about the picture of Sheeran and me." Spence drove from the parking lot onto a road she'd traveled many times before when visiting Fletch. "Right before we left Quantico."

She tapped her forehead to remind him. "Amnesia."

"The way your memory comes and goes can be real annoying."

"Do you think I'm faking it?"

"I didn't say that."

God, he made her furious. She would've slapped his face, but he hadn't shaved this morning and his firm jaw was covered with thick, blond stubble. If she touched him, she'd end up caressing him. He was too damn handsome.

"We don't have time for these spats," she said.

"Agreed."

Today was the fourteenth. The strike on Dallas would probably take place on the sixteenth. If the targeted time was the stroke of midnight, that was only thirty-eight hours from now. She needed to focus, but her memory couldn't immediately reboot after recalling the photo that was part of a larger picture of a formal event at the Kennedy Center. It was no big surprise that the photographer had taken several shots of shapely Raquel Sheeran with her mane of red hair. With Spence at her side, the combined magnificence was blinding.

Angelica wouldn't say that she was jealous of SSA Sheeran, aka Jessica Rabbit. Obviously, Spence was going to enjoy the view that Sheeran put on display. She didn't care that he'd escorted Sheeran to the event, but he'd told her that the photo was a fluke that happened to catch them in the same shot. He'd said they weren't together.

She exhaled an angry huff. "If you had just told me that you dated her before we met, I wouldn't care."

"You said we weren't going to...what did you call it?"

"Spat." Facing ninety degrees away from him, she stared out the front windshield. A narrow two-lane, winding road cut through a snowy forest of pine and conifer. In her peripheral vision, she noticed his large hand gripping the steering wheel, and she thought of how sensitive those paws had been last night when he stroked her inner thigh.

"We'll arrive at our destination soon," he said as he followed the GPS instruction to go right, then right again. "Do you need to call and let anybody know?"

"I talked to Fletch this morning. Your former girlfriend, SSA Sheeran, released him and the boys last night. Fletch was going to stay at his house in town and sleep late."

"She was never my girlfriend," he said.

"That's not what the gossip around the office says. The way I heard it, you went out for three or four months."

"I'm going to say this again, for the last time. I was on assignment in Denver, which is where I met Sheeran. We went out to dinner a couple of times. She invited me to a ski weekend, where we spent the night in the same tiny cabin but not the same bed."

Others in his office had been quick to show

her the photo in a back issue of an FBI publication and to tell her to watch out for Spence. "Were you at the party with her?"

"We came in a limo with four others. I wouldn't call it a date, but we left the event at the same time and rode back to the hotel together."

"And at the hotel?"

"We hugged," he said, "and went to bed in our separate rooms. In the spirit of full disclosure, I was dating another woman at the time."

Hooking up with two women at the same time sounded more like the image of Spence that provided the office with gossip. "If you're so innocent, why does everybody think you're a player?"

"I'm not." Before she could say anything else, he held up his hand for silence. "There's something else I want to tell you."

"Go ahead."

"I kissed SSA Sheeran. I didn't count how

many times, but only twice with tongue. And I touched her breasts." He made a squeezing gesture with his hand, giving a clear indication of how he'd done a bit more than touch. "They're real and very impressive. But she isn't the right woman for me, and I didn't want to lead her on. She's a woman who takes revenge, and I didn't want to lose any of my favorite body parts."

"Why should I believe you?"

"Trust," he said, "is a two-way street."

She'd walked right into that one. He had every right to demand trust from her. If he told her he hadn't slept with the stunning redhead, she had to believe him. "Well played."

"I'm not trying to put one over," he said. "I meant what I said about Sheeran. She's a scary, high-maintenance woman."

Though familiar with the phrase, she asked, "What does high maintenance mean to you?"

"She demands all the attention, all the time. Her tastes are recklessly expensive. Everything has to be perfect. Did you notice that she had her FBI windbreaker tailored? She needs to be pampered. And the poor sucker who falls for her has to live up to her expectations."

"You've given this some thought," she said.

"I grew up poor. Working as a valet and a busboy, I had the chance to study these ladies. They aren't for me."

According to his story, he had still taken the opportunity to feel her impressive breasts. Angelica could hardly blame him.

On the left side of the road, she pointed toward a chestnut-brown house with a deck across the front and tall A-frame gables on either end of a garage. She'd always thought of the gables as peaked eyebrows and the garage as a mouth. The eccentric-looking home suited Professor Fletcher very well.

Tire tracks plowed through the snow on the driveway and disappeared into the garage, but nothing had been shoveled. The accumulation was five or six inches, deeper where the snow had drifted. Anxious to get started with the professor's computer programs, her hand was on the door handle when Spence parked on the road.

"You could drive a bit closer," she said.

He took his gun from the holster. "We'll proceed with caution. Tire tracks into the garage indicate that somebody is inside, and Fletch told you he wasn't coming up here."

Though she hadn't been planning to sneak up on the professor's house, she knew Spence was correct. This would be a short hike through the snow, which meant zipping her parka and pulling on a knit hat. With her gun drawn, she climbed out of the SUV and closed the car door as quietly as possible. She hoped, really hoped, they wouldn't find anything terrible inside.

She had no problem letting Spence take the lead. For a big man, he moved with incredible stealth through the ankle-deep snow. To reach the entrance, they had to climb a zigzag double staircase to the deck. The front door was in the center section between the peaked gables and above the garage.

Her hiking boots gave her good traction, but she slipped halfway up the second staircase. If she hadn't caught the banister, she'd have fallen. The gun fell from her hand.

She mouthed to Spence, "I'll get it."

Near the bottom of the lower staircase, she heard a noise. Someone was nearby. She froze in place.

"Hands up," a deep voice said. "Don't make me shoot."

"It's okay," she said. "I have permission to be here."

"You heard me," the voice said. "Just do it."

With a whoosh, Spence vaulted over the upper banister and landed in the snow beside the stair-case—a dangerous move. He could have broken both legs, but seemed to be unharmed when he stood up straight and aimed his gun.

Until this moment, she hadn't completely forgiven him. But how could she stay angry at a man who naturally reacted like a superhero? He amazed her.

And Spence was definitely in charge. He snapped an order at the other man. "Put the gun down."

"No way am I going to shoot. I was joking around."

She turned. "Is that you, Dunne?"

"Now," Spence said. "Gun on the ground."

"Yeah, sure." He dropped the gun and took a step back. "We cool?"

Dunne and his man bun irritated her. He'd changed from his Hawaiian shirt to a dark green hoodie and an extra-long scarf that dangled almost to his knees. She scowled at him. "What are you doing here?"

"The professor wanted me to help you with his equipment. Some of the setups are weird."

Spence scooped up her gun and handed it to her. To Dunne, he said, "Take us inside. I have questions for you."

"More questions?" he groaned as he led them to the far side of the three-car garage where there was a regular, human-sized door. "At FBI headquarters, I must have talked nonstop for two hours. Big Red had one question after another."

Angelica had to ask. "Big Red?"

"You know who I'm talking about. Special Agent Hottie. The legs on her are enough to make me confess to just about anything."

As Spence herded them through the side garage door that she hadn't known was there, he chided Dunne. "SSA Sheeran is a federal agent. She warrants respect."

Dunne chuckled to himself. "Hey, that wasn't

an insult. I called her *Special Agent* Hottie, didn't I?"

Spence whipped out his cell phone. "I've got her on speed dial. Let's see if she finds your tone respectful."

"Please don't call her," Dunne said. "I'm sorry, really."

"Your sense of humor needs an adjustment. It's not funny to aim a gun at a friend or to call people names. Can you give me a 'yes, sir' on that?"

"Yes, sir."

She climbed the staircase from the basement level to the first floor. The living room furnishings were more appropriate for an office than a space for social occasions. There were desks and worktables and computers all over the place. When Fletch bought this house, he intended for it to be a hideaway where he could work uninterrupted on various projects. It hadn't quite turned out that way. His privacy was hindered by his bad habit of sharing the location with other professors and his students.

She walked through the kitchen and went past the round table where a box of chocolate-flavored breakfast cereal testified to the taste level of Dunne and his buddies. The most remarkable feature of the front room was a wall of windows overlooking a stunning view of the forest, rolling hills and the high peaks beyond.

Spence stepped up beside her. "I didn't realize we were on a cliff."

"This place is full of surprises," she said.

"If there's a way to cover those windows, we should use it. All that glass has to be letting in the cold."

"They're triple pane. Not bad as insulation."

"Also bulletproof," he said.

"Typical," she murmured. "You brought an innocent conversation around to danger."

"Bulletproof is a good thing. Does Fletch have

a reason to be worried about assassination attempts?"

"I sincerely hope not."

How could she think of Fletch as a suspect? He was kind, sweet and would never hurt a flea. Surely, he wouldn't drop a nuke on a major city. But someone had plans for mass destruction, and that individual was someone she'd met.

She had to find this person or these people. But how? Her thoughts didn't naturally center on bullets and assassinations, and her brain still wasn't operating at full throttle. Maybe she wasn't cut out to be a field agent. If she'd been at her desk in Cyber Security headquarters, her stomach wouldn't feel like she'd been whirling in a centrifuge.

Spence whispered her name, and she looked up at him. "You're going to be okay," he assured her.

"What if I can't figure this out?"

"You'll get it. Your cyber buddies at NSA are

working on this, too." He turned his head to look out at the view. "Inhale a deep breath. Take in the beauty. Trust yourself."

Sunlight glistened against the new snow. The sky above the peaks was a pure blue. She could feel herself calming down. "Fletch calls this house his crucible."

"Like the alchemy tool."

She reared back. "I didn't expect you to know that."

"I grew up poor, not uneducated."

"That's not what I meant. I just don't think of alchemy as the kind of thing a man like you would be interested in."

"It's not a favorite topic at tailgate parties," he admitted. "But I understand why your professor wanted a space where he could create."

"Do you ever have that urge?"

He nodded. "Maybe."

"Your undercover work is actually very creative. You might be a good actor."

"Or not." His grin was a bit self-conscious. "Ready to get started?"

She pivoted and marched toward the kitchen, where Dunne was eating his chocolate cereal right out of the box. Needing to work with him rankled, but she'd do anything to save time.

"Show me a computer," she said, "where I can go deep."

"Are you talking about the dark web? Black hat operations? I didn't think you government types went in for that."

"Show me."

In a corner room with two windows and a colorful paisley, he showed her a bank of computers. There were three screens. The one in the middle was extra large.

"These babies suck up a lot of power," Dunne said. "When not in use, we turn them off. There are four linked consoles, and you have to turn them on in order from left to right."

He flicked the switches and little green lights

came on. Though there wasn't a hum, she felt an energy surge.

"What about the screens?" she asked.

"They work the same way. Turn them on from left to right."

She sat in the swivel chair in front of the computers. Leaning forward, she turned on the screens. The two smaller displays came to life, showing pictures of mountain landscapes. The large center screen remained blank.

"What's wrong with it?" she asked.

"It's on." He pointed to the blinking light. "I don't know why it's taking so long to warm up."

A burst of red and yellow exploded across the screen, and then a Grim Reaper carrying a scythe appeared. From the eye sockets of the skull, squiggles crawled like snakes and formed two words in 24-point type: You're Dead.

Chapter Fifteen

Standing in the doorway across the room from the death screen, Spence watched Dunne's reaction. First, there was surprise and then a bright flicker in his eye. A muscle in Dunne's jaw twitched as though holding back a grin. Spence figured that Dunne hadn't expected a Grim Reaper but he wasn't scared by the skull or the threat.

Spence crossed the room to the swivel chair where Angelica sat with her fingers poised above the keyboard. He wanted that grotesque image to be far away from her.

"Turn it off," he growled.

"Not yet. I might be able to trace where it came from."

"I hate it."

"These graphics are nothing." She tilted her head to look up at him. "You don't play computer games, do you?"

Real life was scary enough without searching for additional on-screen thrills. "Can't say that I do."

"Well, some of the gaming images are horrendous. They'll give you nightmares."

She pounced on the keyboard. After a few strokes, the Grim Reaper faded to a box in the upper right corner while the rest of the screen filled with data streams. Whenever he watched her doing her job, he was in awe. His angel was brilliant and beautiful.

His hands dropped to her shoulders, and he massaged. At the nape of her neck, he felt knots of tension and pressed hard against them until they released. She shrugged and gave a soft moan that reminded him of last night in bed.

Without looking up, she asked, "Do you think the threat is meant for Professor Fletch?"

"The computer belongs to him." Taking advantage of an opportunity to confront Dunne, he pointed a finger at the center of his skinny chest. "This could be a warning for you. Who did you tell that you were going to be here?"

"Nobody." He waved his hands as though he could divert Spence's intense scrutiny. "What about her? Somebody might want to hurt her."

"For your sake, I hope not."

Dunne shook his head. The hint of a smile was completely erased from his long, thin face. "What's that supposed to mean? For my sake?"

"Nobody knew we were going to be here but Fletcher. And he told you. That means either you or your mentor are responsible for the image on that screen."

"Not me. There wasn't time. I barely had a

chance to change clothes before I left for the cabin, not enough time to set up complicated graphics."

Spence leaned toward Angelica, who was still tapping at the keyboard. "Is that true? Would it take a long time?"

"Maybe," she said as she shot a glance toward Spence. "I might have mentioned to my dad that we were coming here."

And Sheeran could have figured it out. It was unlikely that Dunne had anything to do with the death head. He knew Angelica would be here and had a grudging respect for her skills, but Spence didn't want to let him off the hook too easily. "You must have told somebody else."

"Nobody." He dug into his pocket, pulled out his cell phone and passed it to Spence. "See for yourself. I didn't call anybody."

"You could have used a burner phone."

"Think again," Dunne said. "I had nothing to do with the Reaper. If you want to know the truth, I'm worried that Fletch might be in danger."

Spence needed to develop a more precise psychology for Dunne—a profile. He was probably in his late twenties, a little younger than Spence but far more immature. Dunne dressed like a student. Yet, there was something about his clothes and his man bun that made Spence think of a disguise. Dunne was different from nerds like Lambert and Heller. He lacked their dedication and their innocence.

"Where do you work?" Spence asked.

"A coffee shop."

"Part-time?"

"That's right," Dunne snapped. "What is this? A job interview?"

A part-time job didn't earn enough money to pay rent. Spence drew the next logical conclusion. "Do you live with Fletch?"

"Congratulations, Secret Agent Man, you figured it out. Fletch is my boyfriend."

Angelica swiveled around in her chair and gave him a congratulatory thumbs-up. "I knew it. You're his type, slim and not too tall. I'll bet you have great hair when you take down that stupid bun."

"Should I say thank you?"

"If I were you," Spence said, "I'd take it. She's not big on compliments."

Behind Angelica, the Reaper image on the screen flashed in another explosion, and then faded into a tame, pleasant picture of a forest glen. The soft, bubbling sound of water rushing in a creek accompanied the image.

He was glad to see the threat disappear. "What happened?"

"It was on a timer," she said. "I went as far as I could in tracing. The best I can figure is that it originated at an internet coffee shop in Reykjavik."

Dunne chuckled. Spence was confused. "Explain."

"The programmer who sent the Reaper is good at covering his or her tracks. He or she made it appear as though the message came from an impossible location." She paused, thought for a moment, and then continued, "Actually, this individual is better than good. They're world-class."

"How do you know?"

"Because he or she is as computer savvy as I am. And I'm incredible." In her swivel chair, she spun in a one-eighty so she was facing the computer screen again. "If you gentlemen will excuse me, I have some web work to do."

Spence hustled Dunne from the room. In the kitchen, Dunne prepared a fresh pot of coffee while Spence rummaged through the fridge until he found the fixings for ham sandwiches. Still thinking about his profile for Dunne, he couldn't decide if this guy was a suspect or a witness.

Dunne presented himself as a facilitator, willing to help when asked. The professor had sent him to open this cabin for them. Dunne had gone to pick up Lambert. He'd carried and displayed the computer image of Heller's murder.

While Spence spread mustard and mayo on slices of bread, he dissected that profile. Sometimes, a facilitator was a nice person who enjoyed helping others, people like the pastor and Trudy. Other times, facilitators were sociopaths who arranged situations to their benefit. He wouldn't be surprised to find that Dunne orchestrated the camera-under-the-door trip to the hotel that he, Lambert and Fletch had made, supposedly to meet with Angelica.

Ironically, it was Dunne who asked the next question. "How long have you and Angelica been dating?"

"Six months."

"Is it serious? Not that I care," he said, "but Fletch adores that girl, talks about her all the time. She was his smartest, most original, cleverest student."

"She likes him, too."

Impatient, he huffed. "So, is it serious?"

Spence knew better than to share personal information with a possible suspect. He and Dunne weren't buddies but adversaries. Instead of declaring his undying love or mentioning the engagement ring he'd been carrying around while waiting for the right moment, Spence gave a noncommittal shrug. "Why do you care? I thought you were gay."

"I go both ways." His upper lip curled in a sneer that he probably thought was derisive. "Don't get me wrong. I'm not conning Fletcher and I really care about him. He's the reason I'm concerned about her. I don't want to see him upset by having his sweetie pie angel end up dead."

Upset seemed like a mild description. "I'm

guessing Fletch didn't feel too bad about Heller's murder."

"He was shocked. His first instinct when I showed him the computer image was to push it away."

Dunne sounded hurt, and Spence had to wonder why. "You didn't like that, the way he ignored the image."

"I had to make him look." He was vehement. "He needed to fix it, to make sense of it."

"Only Fletch could fix it."

"Damn right."

Spence set the plates with ham sandwiches in front of them on the center island. He needed to keep Dunne talking. "But Fletch didn't study the image, didn't go deep enough."

"That's her fault," he said. "Fletcher wanted to consult with Angelica. And—you won't believe this—he wanted to wait until morning."

"You needed to move a lot quicker than that," Spence said, keeping in mind that Dunne supposedly didn't know that the clock was ticking down the minutes to the strike on the sixteenth. "There's a deadline."

Dunne turned away. His mouth zipped into a straight line. Spence could almost see the walls Dunne was building to keep him from getting closer. Good, he'd hit a nerve.

From the guidelines he'd learned in FBI profiling, he had a fuller picture of Dunne. Not only was he emotionally immature but he was sexually confused and looking for a father figure like the professor. As a sociopath, Dunne lacked empathy. Everything was about him and satisfying his needs.

Spence had known sneaky kids like Dunne in foster care. They were fast talkers, friendly when they needed to be, but quick to throw you under the bus if it suited their needs.

Spence fed his ego. "You already figured it out, didn't you? You spotted the clue in that computer image. You're smarter than you look.

You worked out the puzzle faster than the professor or Angelica."

"I haven't got a clue what you're talking about."

But he almost nodded in the affirmative. Spence pushed for more information. "There is a clue, isn't there?"

"How would I know?"

"Show me. You and I can go over the image together."

He could tell that Dunne was tempted. His fingers twitched, and he licked his lips, but he said, "I'm not an expert. I don't know what to look for. Besides, we don't have the computer with the image."

Actually, they did have that computer. Angelica had taken possession and hadn't turned it over to the FBI or to the computer nerds at Peterson AFB. Spence hesitated, not wanting to give Dunne too much information. "What can you tell me without the computer?"

"I suppose I don't need the image to give you the clue. Pay attention, you might learn something."

Spence nodded and said nothing, hoping that if Dunne kept talking, he'd eventually incriminate himself.

"You and Angelica found the body, right?"

Again, Spence nodded. He took a bite of his sandwich and chewed slowly. The ham was bland, nearly flavorless, but the mustard was spicy.

"Did you see any remote cameras in the room?" Dunne asked.

Another nod. "But none of them were hooked up."

"What if…" Dunne paused for dramatic effect. "What if there was a tiny, nearly microscopic camera on the wall behind Heller or in a heating grate or hidden on a bookshelf. Are you following me?"

"Keep going."

"The camera feed could have sent the photo to that computer," he said triumphantly. "Nobody had to be in the room to snap the photo. It was programmed."

"Angelica said the computer took that picture. It wasn't sent forward from anything else."

Dunne flapped his hand dismissively. "She's not infallible, you know. A remote camera feed makes more sense. I bet Heller set it up himself, to record visitors to his apartment."

If Heller had intended to make a record of other people, why would he point the camera at the back of his own head? That was some seriously flawed logic, but Spence didn't point it out. He wanted to keep Dunne engaged and talking. "You could very well be right. Heller must have had somebody working with him. And that person must have picked up the feed."

"Bo Lambert." Like any sociopath worthy of the profile, he was quick to dump the blame on some poor dope like Lambert. "The image of the murder showed up on a computer that belonged in Lambert's office."

"Which was also Heller's office."

"And didn't Lambert already admit that Heller offered him a job? Five thousand bucks for an afternoon?"

"Lambert said he turned down the assignment." Spence believed Lambert's confession that he'd almost gotten involved in Heller's weird scheme because of a long-ago crush on Angelica. Admitting his gullibility had to bring up painful memories.

"What if he was lying?"

It was time to call an end to this sparring match. Spence flipped the tables. "What about your alibi?"

Dunne stuffed his mouth with sandwich, maybe to keep from saying more that made him look worse. He choked out the words. "What about it?"

"The alibi went like this. You and Lambert

and Fletch were together from when you and Lambert picked up the car until after dinner when Lambert found the computer."

"Another reason Lambert has to be the guilty one," Dunne said. "He found the computer."

"But he didn't commit the murder. We can't get around that alibi."

"Well, we weren't joined at the hip." Dunne thrust out his pelvis. "He could have slipped out. Wait, I remember that I took a little nap. That's when he did it. Maybe the camera feed was in his vehicle. And he had enough time to go back to Heller's apartment."

"How far is Heller's apartment from Fletcher's house?"

"I don't know. Maybe fifteen or twenty minutes away."

It was more like ten. Spence had clocked it this morning with Angelica before they headed to the mountains. Dunne had painted himself into a corner. He had time to sneak away from

Fletcher's house and make a round trip to Heller's apartment and back.

In the worst-case scenario, Dunne shot his friend in the back of the head, picked up a computer and snapped a photo before he returned home.

Chapter Sixteen

Spence wasn't altogether sure what Angelica was doing in the corner office with the computers. Shortly after he and Dunne had finished their ham sandwiches and veiled accusations, she'd invited Dunne into her sanctum. She'd needed him to show her how to run the various printers, including an enlarger capable of creating documents that were three feet square. Then Dunne was out, Spence was in, and she asked him to shut the door.

The moment he turned and faced her, she was on him. Her arms twined around his neck. Her body aligned with his as she pressed him against the closed door. She kissed him carefully, still mindful of her split lip. Her tongue delicately explored his mouth, slid across his teeth, and then plunged deeper.

She pulled back. "You taste like mustard."

"Hungry?"

"Only for you."

He wrapped her in his arms and squeezed, crushing her slender body against his chest, stealing her breath, consuming her. He wrestled her feet off the floor, and she coiled her legs around him. He was hard as stone against her.

They shouldn't allow themselves to be distracted. There was important work to be done. If they couldn't decipher the hack at NORAD, a major American city might be destroyed in a fatal strike. And yet, his every thought, every urge, led back to her. He wanted to be inside her, to stay with her for an hour or a day or maybe the rest of his natural life.

When he spoke, his strangled voice caught in

his throat. He didn't sound like himself. "We don't have time."

"I know."

"Have you found anything?" he asked.

"I've got ideas."

"So do I."

He should be telling her that Dunne might be more involved than they'd thought and shouldn't be trusted. Instead, he settled her firmly against his erection. She rubbed herself up and down, creating a warm friction against him. The buttons on his jeans twisted between them. He wanted her to keep going, never to stop.

She threw back her head, and he nuzzled the slender column of her throat. A wild shudder went through her. Gasping, she slid down his body until her feet were firmly planted on the floor.

"I had to do that," she said.

"I'm glad to oblige." He would've been a lot

happier if he'd gotten the same release that she achieved.

"Otherwise," she said, "I would have been too preoccupied thinking about you to concentrate on anything else."

Actually dizzy, he closed his eyes and leaned his back against the door. "How can I help?"

"Give me privacy. I need to pull things together."

He didn't want to go back to the other room with Dunne, especially not now when he was pretty sure the guy was a sociopath. "I'll just sit in the corner and be quiet."

"You make me crazy. You've got to go."

And so, he left.

THAT HAD BEEN two hours ago. During much of that time, he'd been on the phone with Quantico and the local FBI. Dunne had been granted entrance to her locked room, and she'd printed him a copy of the photograph of Heller, which he stuck under Spence's nose.

For a good twenty minutes, Spence studied the picture, noticing titles on books that were visible and squinting at the papers on Heller's desk. Among those papers was one with scribbles. Amid the scribbles was the code that was driving Spence crazy: Y75110.

The code had significance. It told him that Heller was connected to the hacking and the possible strikes. But Spence had already made that link when Trevor told him that Heller had been holding Angelica.

He stalked down the hallway to the corner bedroom. If he stood with his ear to the door, he could hear her plucking at the keys and printing and tearing papers. What the hell?

"Here comes trouble," Dunne announced from the front room. "It's Big Red."

"Sheeran?" Spence straightened his spine. "What's she doing here?"

"I don't know. She's coming up the stairs."

Spence rapped on the door. "Angelica, I need to interrupt."

She whipped the door open and stepped back to give him a full view of the corner office. Along one wall, she'd taped four huge, black-and-white maps of Western United States. The eastern half of the country was on the opposite side. With markers, she'd put in dots of varying colors. The majority were red. The two windows were covered by transparencies that hung over the curtain rods. Thumbtacks fastened several smaller maps and coded charts to the wall in a pyramid pattern. Colored pieces of string attached some of the dots and codes. On a bulletin board, she'd tacked up copies of newspaper articles. It looked like the untidy nest of a giant bird.

"I'm not done," she said.

He shoved the door closed and locked it behind him. Until he could make sense of this chaos, he didn't intend to share with Sheeran. He turned to Angelica. "I'm going to need a little explanation."

"First, I need to tell you about my visit to the dark web." Her mouth twisted in disgust. "It's gross. Every perversion you can imagine has buyers and sellers."

"What did you find out about the hack?"

"I followed a couple of threads that tangled in and out and around. The hacker is offering an auction of six nukes and is demanding a multi-million-dollar payoff. The proof will be at Dallas on the sixteenth."

Somewhere in the back of his mind, he'd been hoping they were wrong. "Our theory is confirmed."

She nodded. "I sent the details and dark web links to my supervisor. Somebody from our office will pose as a buyer and go after the seller. It's the kind of operation they've done before."

"That's not going to help Dallas," he said.

"I'm afraid that's our problem."

He paced in a tight circle. The clutter prevented him from taking a regular-length stride. "Tell me about all this."

"Some of the maps are from the FBI flash drive. Others are from Peterson AFB."

As she explained, she brightened. Leaving the dark web behind, she enjoyed this part of the process—the puzzle solving. She continued, "I've been creating a timeline within each area that shows the original sites for missile silos and how they've changed over the years. New ones were added. Some were decommissioned."

"Why?"

She shrugged. "Why would I know how NORAD makes policy? The warheads taken off-line are aging and might need repairs."

"What I want to know," he said, "is why you set up this craft project with all the color coding?"

"One of the guiding concepts of cryptography is being able to look at a problem from a different perspective."

He was familiar with the idea. "Thinking outside the box."

She took his hand and dragged him into the center of the chaos. "Close your eyes and cover them with your hands."

He recalled last night when he'd guided her in a meditation exercise. This might be her version of the same thing. "They're covered."

"When I count to three, open them. See what object catches your focus."

She counted, and he peeked. His gaze went directly to the letter *C* on a map of the Western states. He moved closer to interpret the symbol, which appeared to be a designated sector in northern Colorado with two red-dot missile silos.

"Reminds me of C4ICBM," she said. "C4 might not mean explosives. Maybe it's a location."

From down the hall, he heard the husky rumble of SSA Sheeran calling his name. "I don't know why she's here," he said.

"Her reasons could be purely professional," she said with a tight-lipped smile. "Maybe she's got good news."

"Come with me."

"I'd rather stay here," she said. "I'm getting close. I can feel it."

She pushed him toward the door and closed it behind him. He heard the click as she engaged the lock.

STILL GAZING AT the door, Angelica closed her eyes, squinted hard and popped her eyelids open. She'd been hoping her intense concentration would make SSA Sheeran disappear, but that wasn't going to happen. She could hear the sexy tone of the redhead's voice in the hallway as she talked to Spence.

Shuffling through the mess of papers scattered on the floor, Angelica returned to her swivel chair behind the desk and typed a message to Bo Lambert. He'd been helping her find one of the first maps of the missile sites, circa 1955 when the Santa Claus tracking program started.

She knew the map existed because her dad showed it to her. Sixty years ago, when he was a kid and his father had been in the air force, they tracked Santa on a flight map. Every Christmas, her father repeated that tradition with his own children.

At the time, she hadn't been aware that the dots on the map represented missile silos that held nuclear warheads. Her dad certainly didn't tell her. But she was a curious kid and had figured it out.

Unlike the maps she'd taped to the wall, the early versions couldn't be readily accessed. Those records were on computers that weren't compatible with present-day technology. To find them, Lambert had to make a physical search in the archives at Peterson AFB.

Lambert emailed her back. He couldn't find the maps she needed and suggested that those records might be filed in the Cheyenne Mountain Complex. She needed to go inside the Complex. But first, she'd call her dad. He was the world's most organized person and could probably put his hands on the family Christmas map in five minutes.

Again, she squeezed her eyes shut and popped them open. The lines and contours on the maps blended like an abstract painting. Thinking outside the box, she played with the Y75110 code on the computer, breaking it apart to read: Y75-110 and Y7-5110. When she squinted, the "5" looked like an *S*.

Before she pushed away from the desk, she went through the shutting down sequence and made a call to her dad. When she told him what she needed, he responded—as she'd expected—

that he knew exactly where to find the Santa Claus tracking maps. She asked him to meet her at Peterson AFB. If she found what she was looking for, Angelica might need to borrow military equipment and personnel.

Down the hallway, she spotted SSA Sheeran leaning against the center island in the kitchen and lecturing about the murder of Lex Heller. Occasionally, Sheeran referred to a computer tablet for the specifics.

"Cause of death is a .45 caliber bullet to the skull. Gunshot residue indicates the barrel of the weapon was close to the head when fired. No sign of a struggle. There won't be an autopsy for the next four or five days, longer if they send the body to the Colorado Bureau of Investigation in Denver."

"Why would they do that?" Spence asked.

"Who knows? It's not my jurisdiction. The local cops have got their reasons." She turned her head toward Angelica and tilted her sunglasses down to peek over the top of the lenses. "Good afternoon, Agent Thorne."

"Same to you." She nodded a hello, not offering to do another strength-sapping handshake. "I'm sorry to interrupt, but we need to go."

"Where are you headed?"

"Family business," she said. "We're going to catch up with my dad at Peterson."

"Great," Sheeran said. "I'll come with you. I've always wanted to meet General Thorne."

Angelica didn't believe that for one hot minute, and she didn't want to get stuck spending the rest of the day with the SSA. But they all were on the same team, and she couldn't refuse. "You can follow us."

She returned to the office to pick up her computer. While she was there, she figured that she might as well put together some of these maps. She took the maps of Western United States down from the wall and rolled them into a cylinder.

For one last time, she closed her eyes and popped them open. Her gaze landed on the code that had become so familiar to her: Y75110.

This time, for the first time, she saw it differently. They weren't numbers but letters. The "5" was an *S*. The first "1" was a capital *I*, and the second was an *L*. The code spelled a word: *SILO*. There were seven silos. The launch missiles and nuclear warheads inside the silos were the threat.

Chapter Seventeen

During the drive from Fletcher's cabin to Peterson AFB, Angelica reached across the console and held Spence's hand. She was cold, chilled to the bone with the fear of what might happen if she couldn't figure out how these missile silos were being manipulated. The warmth of his grasp reminded her that most of the world wasn't like the dark web. Most people weren't willing to launch a nuke and destroy an entire city, not even for a multimillion-dollar payoff.

At first, she'd been too tense to speak, but Spence wasn't going to let her sit in the passenger seat like a worried lump. He poked her with one question after another until he had the whole story.

"Seven missile silos," Spence said to summarize, "are going on sale to the highest bidder."

"Make that six," she corrected. "The nuclear warheads in one of them will have been used to wipe out Dallas."

"You're saying that these missile silos differ from all others in the system. They don't fall under NORAD's umbrella of protection with redundant computer programs and firewalls."

"Correct."

"Somehow," he said, "the bad guys have gotten control."

"Correct, again."

He glanced over at her. "You've got to breathe, angel."

"C-c-can't," she stammered. "Too scared."

"Me, too."

She gazed at his profile, still gorgeous. He didn't sound frightened. His hand wasn't shaking the way hers was. Though he might be quaking like an aspen under the surface, he appeared to have himself under control. It was an act he'd probably done many times on life-and-death assignments.

Though she lacked his years of experience, she had determination. She'd figure out how to eliminate the threat. She had to do it. The alternative was too terrible.

Spence had told her to breathe, and she concentrated on inhaling and exhaling deeply and slowly, trying to suppress her rising sense of panic. It was late afternoon on the fourteenth. The day was fading fast. Tomorrow there would only be one more day before the strike.

Approaching the base, they ran into heavy traffic. Even in a midsize city like Colorado Springs, rush hour was a factor. She glared at the "Kiss a Cowboy" bumper sticker on the truck in front of them. "Can't we go any faster?"

"We're making good time," he said. "We've already caught up to Sheeran and Dunne."

"She's supposed to be behind us. I told her to follow."

"Not her style," he said.

Sheeran and Dunne made an exceedingly odd couple. "Why did she bring him along?"

"I asked her to. It's one of those keep-your-enemies-close things. He needs monitoring. At best, Dunne's a sociopath. I don't want to contemplate the worst."

"He can't be totally worthless," she said. "Fletch likes him, and he's a good judge of character."

"Okay, but I'm warning you, as my partner, to be careful around Dunne."

"Another threat," she murmured through a clenched jaw. Danger seemed to be coming from every direction. "I wish I had more help."

"What about your team at NSA? Isn't there anything they can do?"

"They're doing as much as they can, prowling on the dark web, using undercover identities."

"Tell me how that works," he said. "How do you and your cyber buddies go undercover without leaving your desk?"

"It's similar to what you do." She gave his hand a squeeze. "We change our usernames and disguise our identifiable patterns."

"What kind of patterns?"

"Think of when you do undercover work," she said. "You might wear a different style of clothes, maybe dye your hair and put on an accent. You develop a new backstory. Right?"

"You got it."

"People have online personalities, too. Each person inputs data differently. Their language differs. Even the keystrokes are unique. When you go undercover in the cyber world, you have to conceal your computer personality."

"Have you ever been undercover?"

"Sure. My favorite fake identity spends a lot

of time on porn sites, setting honey traps." As she grinned, she realized that talking to him was relaxing her. "My username for her is CherryPi, an oversexed math teacher who likes to see how things add up."

"Give me an example of how that works."

"Here's a story problem. If you have five men and four women, how can you put together three threesomes?"

"Not bad."

"I wanted something sexier but all the fun smutty names were already taken."

"I can't believe I didn't know this about you. CherryPi, huh?" He lifted her hand to his lips and brushed a kiss across the knuckles. "Are you good at talking dirty?"

"Only on the computer," she said. "So don't get your hopes up."

For a few miles, they were quiet, and she didn't mind. This wasn't the static, nervous emptiness she'd felt after she'd discovered the threat was real and she might be the only one who could stop it. Right now, the atmosphere was still, almost peaceful. She listened to the soft jazz he was streaming. Spence was skilled at all forms of relaxation. Being with him helped her mentally gather her resources and prepare for whatever might happen—even though she didn't completely trust him.

"Why did Sheeran come to Fletch's cabin?" she asked.

"Those words sound like trouble," he drawled. "I don't want to hear that you're thinking she was driven wild by unrequited lust and had to be in the same room with me."

"It never crossed my mind." Maybe the thought had occurred to her. But when he said the words out loud, they sounded completely ridiculous. "I've been emailing with the computer guy in their office, Agent Tapper, and he didn't mention Sheeran's visit."

"She's mad and doesn't want me to be the

boss. Remember what I said about high maintenance?"

"Keep her away from me at Peterson."

"Why me?" He groaned. "I'd rather go head-to-head with a drug cartel than attempt to manage a situation between two strong women."

"Am I that scary?"

"If you think I'm going to answer that question, you're dreaming."

Following the signs, he made a left and drove the SUV to the entry gates outside the base. SSA Sheeran had arrived before them, gained entrance and sat waiting in her vehicle on the other side of the gatehouse.

Angelica was ready to show ID, but the sentry at the gatehouse gave her a huge smile and raised the barrier without being asked. Had her father arranged this?

The sentry bounded up to her window. "It's been a while. How are you doing, Selena?"

That explained it. "Selena is my twin. I'm Angelica."

He made eye contact with Spence. "True story?"

"She's Angelica." He held up his shield. "We're FBI."

"Go on through," the sentry said. "Tell Selena that Garret Riley says hi."

Her twin sister made an impression wherever she went. This time, it was positive. A good omen, Angelica decided. She directed Spence through the base to a beige brick building next to a hangar. Her dad's red pickup was parked outside.

Angelica tucked the cylinder of maps under her arm and marched through the double doors. Spence, SSA Sheeran and Dunne came behind her, which made her feel as conspicuous as a drum majorette leading a parade. She'd rather slip in and out of the place where her dad had worked for years without being noticed. She was the quiet twin, the one who always did well and didn't expect to be noticed.

At the front desk, the gray-haired woman looked up from her computer, studied Angelica and then beamed. "I thought I heard something about you being in town."

Rounding the desk, Angelica gave the ample Mrs. Dean a hug and inhaled the scent of snickerdoodle cookies that emanated from the brown cardigan she wore every day, no matter what the weather. "I thought you were going to retire."

"And leave my flyboys to fend for themselves?" she said with a chuckle.

Spence joined them and introduced himself, earning a pat on the cheek from Mrs. Dean. SSA Sheeran and Dunne weren't so polite.

"Your dad is waiting in the conference room." Mrs. Dean pointed down the corridor. "Unless you're fond of sludge, I advise against drinking the coffee he attempted to make."

On the table in the long room with a wall of

windows facing a runway, her dad had already spread out his yellowed, worn, much-creased maps that looked ancient enough to belong to the Pirates of the Caribbean. With his hands clasped behind his back, General Peter Thorne paced in front of the table. His bushy eyebrows scowled at her. He gave Spence a nod and the same for Dunne. Raquel got a rise from the brows.

The SSA slipped off her sunglasses and held out her hand as she introduced herself and told him that she'd heard so much about him. Instead of her usual bone-crushing handshake, she grasped lightly and allowed her fingers to linger as she leaned closer to him. What was her angle? Knowing General Peter Thorne was a boost for anyone who had political aspirations. What was Sheeran trying to pull?

"It's always nice to hear compliments for my family. Who's been talking to you about my dad?" Angelica asked.

"Someone close to me," she said with a sexy toss of her red curls. "My papa served under General Thorne."

"You were an air force brat?"

"Just like you."

"Later, we'll talk." Angelica had neither time nor inclination to bond with Raquel Sheeran right now. They shared a background but not much else. At the table, she concentrated on the maps that showed a large swath of Colorado and Wyoming. She carefully smoothed a frayed corner where one of her brothers or her sister had drawn a picture of Santa in his sleigh.

She asked her dad, "Did you get these flight maps from Grandpa?"

"Sure did. He first showed them to me in 1959." He tossed a chipper little grin to SSA Sheeran. "My pop was an aviator, like me. I had hopes for my youngest boy going into the air force and making it three generations."

"I have my pilot's license," Angelica reminded

him. "So does Selena. We're carrying on the family tradition."

"But flying isn't your livelihood."

"These maps," she said, "were they generated through aerial photography?"

He nodded. "They were used by NORAD. You see those blue circles? Those are missile silos. Santa wouldn't want to fly too close to those."

The map suited her needs perfectly. It was one of the oldest she'd seen that came from direct photography. With Spence's help, she compared the placement of the missiles on the Santa map and on a more recent rendition.

The scale didn't match, and the triangulation created a different slant. Also, the markings on the old maps were faded. This was a tedious exercise, and she was glad SSA Sheeran was keeping her dad occupied. Dunne stared out the window at a helo as the rotor started the swirl before liftoff.

She wasn't 100 percent sure what she was looking for on the maps, which made the finding more of a challenge. Finally, she looked up, met Spence's gaze. Quietly, she said, "It's not what you see, but what you don't."

"What's that mean?"

"A discrepancy." She pointed to similar areas on two different maps. "A missile silo that showed up on the older map was not on the newer."

"Are you sure?" he asked.

"Would you go to the front desk and get a magnifying glass from Mrs. Dean?"

When he strode from the room, her dad and SSA Sheeran huddled in closer. Though Angelica's hopes were soaring, she didn't want to say too much. After all, this was a top secret investigation.

Her dad glowered. "What's the big deal?"

"Until I'm sure, I can't talk about it."

"You can tell me," he said. "I have Level One Security clearance."

"We just want to help," Sheeran said.

There was value in having other people look for anomalies, and she trusted her dad. "I'm sorry, SSA Sheeran. I have to ask you to leave and take Dunne with you."

When the others were in the hall, she gestured for her dad to come closer. With her finger, she drew a circle around the missile silo on the older map and the same area on the newer. "Compare these two maps and tell me how they're different."

Even with her directions, it took a moment for him to notice that the silo was not present on the more recent map.

"It didn't just vanish," her dad said. "Those silos are mostly underground and not meant to stand out, but they are solid installations."

"Maybe it was decommissioned," she said.

"That's how our nuclear treaty agreements

are supposed to be going. We're supposed to take a bunch out of active deployment every year." He gave an uncharacteristic grin. "You know what they call those unactive warheads? Zombie nukes."

Angelica knew she'd have to do more research to figure out which silos had been decommissioned and which were under repair. Most of that work could be done on her computer.

Spence returned with the magnifying glass, and she used it to study the newer map where the silo should have been. A suspicious mound of dirt and rocks drew her attention. The top of the silo could easily be camouflaged.

She passed the magnifier to Spence. "What do you think?"

He scanned the area and concentrated on the same mound that she'd noticed. When he looked up, he shook his head. "I can't tell for sure."

"I know a way."

She took out her cell phone. Even after she

moved back East, Angelica kept up her certifi-
cation. She'd earned her pilot's license before
she graduated from high school.

At a moment's notice, she could be ready for
takeoff.

Chapter Eighteen

Spence jammed his long legs into the narrow space for the copilot's seat in the Piper Cub. He'd flown in small planes before, but nothing as tiny as this. If he stretched out his arms, he could touch both sides of the empennage at the same time. The interior cabin wasn't much bigger than a bathtub.

When Angelica suggested taking a plane to check out the missile silo, which was a little more than a hundred miles away, he'd envisioned a private jet and a possible opportunity to join the mile-high club. On their way across Peterson AFB to the hangars, they passed several sleek, good-looking aircrafts, and she'd teased him by telling him that she was qualified to fly this one or that one. Then they found the guy who'd taught her to fly, and he turned over the keys to the Piper. There was nothing luxurious about this single-propeller plane.

She finished her preflight check and climbed aboard. "With those heavy-duty tundra tires, we can land anywhere."

Though he was fairly certain he wouldn't like her answer, he asked, "When you say land anywhere, what does that mean?"

"When we hit the spot we're looking for on GPS, we drop from the sky and come in for a landing on any flat space."

"Not an airfield?"

"Nothing to worry about, I've flown this little Piper all over the mountains for cross-country skiing and down to Albuquerque for the balloon races and up to Wyoming for the rodeo."

Still pondering the idea of dropping out of the sky, he asked, "Is this safe?"

"Sure." She fiddled with the dials on the console in front of her seat. He was tucked behind her, not so much a copilot as a no-pilot. She continued, "I'll get the GPS set for our missile silo coordinates and off we go. I'd like to get there before the sun goes down so we can make a good, thorough search."

She started the propeller, and he watched the blades slicing the air in front of the windshield. The noise was loud and irritating, reminding him of a lawn mower, and he was happy when she handed him a headset with a microphone attached. With the earphones in place, they could talk to each other.

"Can you hear me?" she asked.

"Loud and clear."

"Get ready for takeoff."

After a short, fast taxi down the runway, they were airborne. Though they were enclosed in the cabin, he sensed the wind rushing around them as they ascended. The elevation wasn't a problem for him. He liked heights and loved the way sunset gilded the edges of the clouds and the rim of the Sangre de Cristo mountain range. The sky took on that delicate rose color that could never really be described.

"There are no words," he said. "Flying into a sunset is pure magic."

"I'm glad you like it."

They bounced over the rough currents. His gut churned. He'd spoken too soon about the magic. If he hadn't been on the verge of throwing up, he would have asked her to turn back and let him out. A parachute was preferable to the jostling, not that there was any way he could leverage his big body to leap from this plane. He was stuck, trapped, uncomfortable and wondering how it was possible to feel claustrophobic while blasting through the sky like a cannonball.

This might be the perfect moment to talk to her about trust. He deserved relationship points for this plane ride. Literally, he had put his life in her hands with nothing more than a pilot's license and an assurance from a grizzled old man at Peterson AFB that she could soar like a hawk. Spence believed in Angelica so much that he'd volunteered for stomach-churning agony.

He seized control of himself. This was his meditation challenge, and he could breathe his way through the inner turmoil. He closed his eyes, concentrated. When he could look around again, he took in the positive beauty and dismissed the gut-wrenching discomfort.

He heard her voice in his ear. "How are you doing?"

"Good," he said, convincing himself. "When we land, what's the plan?"

"We need to search for the missile silo. It's possible that the map my dad has isn't accurate."

"It's a photograph," he said. "Taken in the late 1950s, obviously before Photoshop. And why would anybody add a missile silo to a picture?"

"I trust the map."

"It's possible that we'll search and find signs that the silo has been deactivated."

"Such a waste," she said. "I've heard that people are buying the old missile silos and renovating them into living spaces."

For him, it was hard to believe that anyone would voluntarily live underground without natural light. He shuddered. The Piper took a big bounce, and Spence did some controlled breathing.

He needed something to distract him. "Suppose we find the silo, what does it mean?"

"It's a physical indication of a problem in the computer system." Her shoulders shrugged. "In short, it's evidence. This missile silo was erased from the maps and the computer records. It's gone off-line, which means NORAD doesn't control the launch system."

"Let me see if I've got it," he said. "The bad guys who are selling these nukes on the dark web have control of weapons that supposedly don't exist."

"I need to verify with the computer records," she said, "but that's the basic plot."

Altering a computer program was something he could understand, but he was having a hard time with the concept of physically erasing the missile silos. "The military doesn't drop off these warheads and abandon them. There are launch crews who handle several installations. The way I understand it, these are the guys who make the final decision to push the button."

"They're called missileers," she said. "It's a specialized job in the air force."

The way she'd outlined the plot to steal seven nukes required a plan that was put into effect a long time ago. "In the late fifties and early sixties, the perpetrators had to disguise the locations without anybody knowing."

"And change the computer programs," she said. "We're talking about primitive machines and software. That's what makes this plan nearly unstoppable. Even if we find the nukes, we have to figure out how the old computers worked."

"That's your department."

"Hold on to your seat," she said. "We're here."

She swooped from the sky and guided the Piper toward a gravel road that was barely visible in the dusk. Aiming for a road seemed more sensible than testing their luck on a field with splotches of snow.

Every muscle in his body tensed. He trusted her, believed in her and her abilities. He loved her. This wasn't the first time he'd thought those words or said them, but her amnesia had given him a restart. This time—when he told her—it might be the only time she remembered.

He wanted to make it special with a proposal of marriage and a diamond ring.

The tundra tires of the Piper made contact with the gravel road and they bounced several yards before coming to a complete stop. He couldn't wait to get out of the plane. When his feet hit the ground, his legs wobbled. He lurched forward, telling himself to shake it off. At the same time, his meditative side—the part of him that focused on breathing and sensitivity—was grateful beyond belief.

Both sides wanted her. He flung his arms around her shoulders. "You're amazing."

"Thanks." She snuggled against him. "Flying was never a big deal in my household."

They'd grown up in different worlds. He hadn't taken a commercial flight until he left the foster care system for college. Sometimes, he thought her father was right, and he wasn't good enough for Angelica. The only way to find out was to ask her. After they completed this assignment, he'd propose. That seemed fair enough. All he needed to do before claiming her as his bride was to save the world.

She pointed to a stand of trees in the middle of an open field. "That's a landmark. The silo is near that."

"How near?"

"It's hard to tell from an aerial photo," she said.

"Does this land belong to anybody?"

"I don't know."

He figured it was a good sign that the field wasn't marked off by a barbed wire fence. The road she'd used to land was actually a long straight driveway leading to a ramshackle house that looked like it hadn't been inhabited in years. Colorado might pride itself on being the epicenter of new growth with a constant influx of new residents, but there were still desolate places like this relatively flat area.

He followed her as she trekked across the

field. Though the land was cold and frozen, the weather system that brought the snow hadn't extended this far south. When they reached the trees, she made a left and followed the meanderings of a creek that was little more than a trickle.

His sense of direction was pretty good and he'd studied the contours of the land on the maps. He jumped the creek. "This way."

Approaching a rise in the land that marked the edge of a forest, he looked to the right. The last streaks of sunset were almost gone, and he pulled out a wide-beam flashlight.

She added a Maglite of her own. "It's going to be hard to find anything in the dark."

"A missile silo doesn't just disappear."

After all these years, tire tracks or indentations from heavy equipment would be long gone. Nature reclaimed objects that were left standing. Technology had been developed to x-ray the earth and see what was below the surface, but there wasn't time for that kind of search. By this time tomorrow, there would be only a few hours left before the deadline on the sixteenth.

She pointed her flashlight beam at a mound of earth that had looked suspicious on the aerial photography maps. "I think we should dig."

Easier said than done, the top layer of earth was frozen and they didn't have a real good idea what they were looking for. "Did you bring a shovel?"

"I'm sure there's something in the back of the plane."

The gallant thing to do would be to offer to search for it, but he had no desire to squeeze himself into the tiny Piper any sooner than he had to. Dropping to his knees beside the mound, he said, "You find the shovel. I'll start digging."

He pulled on his gloves, aimed the flashlight so he could see what he was doing and clawed into the frozen earth. His fingers barely made a dent. Without a shovel, this would be slow going. He contented himself with clearing the rocks and other debris.

She returned with the shovel—one of those flimsy collapsible tools that campers used. "Find anything?"

"No, but I agree with you. This is the most likely spot for the silo. I see subtle differences in the vegetation, and it makes me think this soil has been disturbed and then replaced."

"Would it still be different after so many years?"

"It might have been reopened more recently." The seeds to this crime were planted many years ago, but the current plot required awareness of the sites and the technology. "They needed to run checks on the missile and warheads inside."

She nodded. "How do you know so much about vegetation?"

"Searches for hidden graves. Some of the work at so-called body farms was pioneered in

Colorado." Forensic anthropologists spent years deciphering their scientific studies of body decomposition and placement at different burial levels. "Not a fan."

"I've heard about the body farms. When I was in high school, a local aerial photographer found the hidden grave of a woman who had gone missing two years earlier. The earth was concave and the flowers different."

He took the shovel from her and stabbed into the mound. After the outer crust was broken, the dirt crumbled easily. If he'd been using a good shovel instead of this collapsible tool, he would have made faster progress, but the physical exercise satisfied his need to feel useful. She might be the brains in this partnership, but when it came to digging a hole, he was needed.

He plunged the blade of the shovel deep and heard a metallic clunk. Pulling back, he repeated the gesture. He had definitely hit something solid.

"I can't believe it," Angelica whispered. Her tone was reverent, as though singing in Trudy's choir. "This is it. We've found the silo."

"We'd better be sure."

He continued to dig, pulling up large chunks of earth. The clang of the metal shovel against the top of the missile silo echoed in the night. "New problem," he said. "What are we going to do with this? We can't just leave it here, exposed."

"And we don't know who we can trust at NORAD," she said. "Until we've found all seven installations, it's better to keep the traitors in the dark."

"Right," he said, still digging. "If we show our hand too soon, they might set off a nuke to prove that they can."

He'd uncovered enough of the round metal lid on a short concrete base to be satisfied that he'd found the silo. He threw down the shovel and stepped back. "I have people I can talk to at Quantico. We need to get experts out here to deactivate the warheads."

"Until someone else arrives, we'd better wait."

He slung his arm around her waist and pulled her close for a long, thorough kiss. He glanced toward the tiny airplane. If there had been more room, they could have gotten cozy in there. It might still work. He might be able to cram himself into the back. "Does it count for the mile-high club if the plane is on the ground?"

"Why would we try? When I went looking for the shovel, I found some lovely camping gear, including a tent and thermal sleeping bags that are probably good for subzero weather."

"That's what I love about Colorado. People here are ready to camp, 24/7."

"Not everybody is outdoorsy."

Growing up on the street, he was outside all the time, finding an escape from a usually over-crowded home. He considered a vacant lot on the corner to be the great outdoors. But that wasn't his choice.

While he got busy on his cell phone, she set up a little nest using a tent, sleeping bags and a high-powered lantern. When she finished, she gave him a sexy wave, crawled into the tent and closed the flap.

His supervisory agent was enthusiastic about what they'd uncovered and understood the need for their investigation to be kept secret from everybody in Colorado. He promised to put things in motion and would call back with further questions and instructions.

Spence ended the call and approached the pup tent. He opened the flap. Inside, Angelica had zippered the thermal sleeping bags together and crawled inside.

"Don't make me wait any longer," she said.

"Or else?"

"I'll shred you like a cougar."

In the glow of the lantern, he saw that her arm

was bare. Stretched out beside her, he pulled back the sleeping bag. Naked, she welcomed him with a teasing growl.

She was his favorite breed of wildlife.

Chapter Nineteen

Why hadn't they killed me? Angelica found herself asking that question over and over as she and Spence turned the missile silo over to a team of specialists. These missileers from the air force would disarm the ICBM's, deactivate the nukes and make the silo disappear again.

While she and Spence returned to Peterson AFB, the steady hum of the engine on the single-prop Piper relaxed her mind. Again, she considered the issue that Spence had raised early in their investigation. It made sense for the men who abducted her to kill her, to eliminate the threat. *Why am I still alive?*

She was exceedingly happy that they hadn't done the rational thing but couldn't help wondering why they dropped her off. According to Trevor, the thugs had been specifically instructed not to harm her.

After they landed, they came back to the hotel to catch some zees and regroup. Food was a priority. They'd ordered room service for another late-night meal. Sitting at the table in their hotel suite, she forked a bite of salad from the room service plate. She'd ordered blackened salmon, and it looked delicious. Spence ignored his healthy salad and gnawed on spare ribs. He'd been brilliant at the missile site. She'd come to expect his expertise in all things sensual, and he'd heated up their impromptu campsite in many amazing ways. But he'd also proved himself to be efficient and well-organized.

After he made a series of phone calls, it had taken less than two hours for the missileer experts to arrive. Under the supervision of an air force intelligence officer, they went right to work. Other teams were ready to roll as soon as they discovered the other sites.

Though she hoped the black hats would never know they'd been there, she realized that these were computer experts who would surely notice that one of their missiles had been deactivated. That was only one of many concerns.

"As soon as we're done eating," Spence said, "we'll get started on the other maps."

"Finding the other six won't be as hard as locating the first one." Other phone calls he'd made while they were waiting had recruited several unimpeachable researchers to compare the maps. She'd sent copies as soon as they landed at Peterson AFB. "You're really good at delegating."

"Call it a lazy man's skill. The more work other people take on, the less I have on my plate."

Lazy was the last word she'd use to describe

him. With nothing but a cell phone, he'd mobilized a national research project that might prevent a nuclear strike. She checked the time on her cell phone. "Almost midnight."

"Tomorrow is the last day before the strike."

"What if they figure out what we're doing and make their move earlier?"

He cringed. "We have to hope and pray that they don't."

So much could go wrong. They might not find all the sites, even with teams of researchers. The deactivation of the nukes could be mishandled.

"We need to go to Cheyenne Mountain." The only surefire way to stop a launch was for her to reassert the computer protocols. "I need to tap into their computer system from the sixties."

"Can't you do it from a different machine?"

"The modern computers don't speak the same language as the early models."

And she didn't mind entering the Complex. Going inside was always exciting from a scientific standpoint even though the atmosphere made her nervous. The hollowed-out mountain had been constructed during a paranoid era to hold and preserve the nation's most dangerous secrets concerning military weaponry. It was a fortress, intimidating.

But she needed their old computers. If she could get them up and running, she could take the missiles off-line herself. "The Complex is probably on high alert."

"Not because of us," he said. "I made it clear that none of this information was to be shared with the people who work at Peterson or Cheyenne Mountain or the local FBI."

"What about the missileers? Those men are air force."

"And we're holding them in safe houses and top secret locations until this is over." He chewed the last shred of rib meat from the bone. "You've barely touched your food."

"I'm worried," she admitted.

Why am I still alive? Lex Heller and the bad guys had gone to a great deal of trouble to abduct her, pick her brain and give her amnesia. If they truly wanted to keep their plans secret, why would they risk leaving her alive?

Someone was protecting her. The conclusion was inescapable. A person who cared about her had stepped in and ordered that she be spared. She could only think of two men who filled that bill: Professor Morris Fletcher, her first mentor; and her dad.

There was more evidence against those two. While abducted, she'd overheard someone refer repeatedly to "the old man." Again, Fletch and her father fit the bill. And, most damning of all, the long-ago hiding of the missile silos had to be done by someone who worked with NORAD and was active in the early sixties.

Elbow on the table, she rested her chin on her fist and poked at her salmon with the other hand. "Who do you think did this?"

"Dunne played a part. I'm sure about that."

"Why?"

"He shows sociopathic tendencies. I suspect he murdered Heller. His alibi is bogus. He was pushing the computer photo of Heller's body, trying to convince me it was *not* taken by the killer."

"He's innately creepy," she said. "I'll agree to that, but I'm not sure he's a murderer."

"And I think he shot his friend and took the computer picture to use as a sort of trophy. When I interviewed him, he was quick to throw Lambert under the bus. Dunne is not a nice guy." He took a long drink of water. "But he's definitely not a mastermind."

She agreed. "I want to find the person behind the curtain, the instigator. Who set this operation in motion? Who's in control?"

He reached for her plate. "If you're not going to eat, I'll take your fries."

"Go ahead. I'm not hungry. You might as well take the salmon, too."

"Fish—" he pulled a face "—yuck."

"You sound like a kid."

"I swear I'm a grown man, fully grown." His eyelids lowered to half-mast, and there was something sexy about the way he looked at her. He stroked the dark blond stubble on his chin. "Do you want me to shave?"

"Leave the beard."

"It makes me outdoorsy." He patted his cheek. "Like the Colorado dudes you grew up with."

"I never knew anybody like you."

"Ditto."

Her finger stroked her lip, which was mostly healed. They'd been careful about kissing too hard, and she was ready for that caution to end. "Leave the beard. I'm curious to see what it feels like."

"Let me show you."

He rose from the table and took her hand in

an absurdly courtly gesture. Now she had an appetite. She wanted him.

She stood, stepped into his embrace and went up on her tiptoes to rub her cheek against his stubble. The texture was interesting. Not exactly sandpaper, but it was a little prickly. "Doesn't feel like fur."

"Maybe if it was longer..."

"Up to you." She wasn't crazy about beards but didn't totally hate them. His seemed to grow fast.

He trailed the back of his hand along her throat. "Maybe my stubble would feel better in the hot tub."

"I'd feel better," she said. "Let's do it."

In a matter of moments, they had the water heated and the jets pulsing. The hot tub area was an addition to the hotel bathroom and had windows on two sides. They were up high enough so they could look down on the lights of Colorado Springs and still have full privacy. Spence hadn't bothered with a bathrobe. He shed his clothes and strolled around naked and confident. *Well, why wouldn't he be?*

She was more self-conscious. She tested the water with her toe, allowed the robe to slip from her shoulders and climbed in. As she lowered herself into the steaming, churning water, she felt his gaze resting upon her, studying her every move as though he'd never seen her before.

On the opposite side, he glided into the water. "How much do you remember about us?"

"I've been so busy trying to concentrate on the investigation that I haven't tried to put together a chronology."

"First date," he said.

"I know we started dating about six months ago after we worked together on an assignment. And I remember that we both hesitated because we thought it wasn't smart to date a person you worked with."

"We were never supposed to be on the same case," he said. "Never again."

"Oops."

He ducked his head under the water, bobbed to the surface and shook like a dog. "You already told me you remembered *Camelot.*"

The jets massaged her arms and shoulders. The bruise on her hip only ached a little bit. Another memory resonated in her mind. It was when he told her that he loved her for the first time. They'd just finished having sex, and the moment hadn't been terribly romantic. It took her a few days to respond. "Why are you asking about this?"

"If you've forgotten things about our relationship, it'll seem like the first time when I do them again."

"I can't believe this." She shook her head. "You want a do-over? A free pass?"

"I want to do this right." He scooted close to

her and lifted her palms to his cheeks. "Touch the beard."

"You're right. It's much softer when we're wet."

"And it'll be even better when we kiss."

She joined her mouth with his and tasted his lips. Gently, his hands dived to stroke the most sensitive parts of her body. She returned the favor.

"I never forgot this," she whispered. "I remember the very good, exceptionally good sex."

She was happy to splash and grope and make love until they fell into bed exhausted. They needed the sleep. Tomorrow was the last day before the deadline.

Chapter Twenty

By seven o'clock the next morning, they were both up and dressed and steeped in information. At the table, Spence shuffled through their collection of maps, reading the location coordinates and talking to his Quantico SSA on the cell phone. He knew they were behind schedule and hoped their frantic efforts weren't futile. Last night, the researchers had only located three more of the off-line silos. Not good enough.

Three missiles were still unaccounted for. He recalled the words Angelica had spoken when he directed her through the guided meditation: *It only takes one.*

One nuclear strike would destroy a city, kill thousands and poison thousands more. The surrounding farmland and forests would take years to come back from the devastation. He and his supervisor had discussed the possible evacuation of Dallas, but Angelica talked him out of it, pointing out that the black hats could change their target.

She continued to pour over the maps, comparing them sector by sector. She'd gone from using her dad's map to another from a few years later. She'd alerted the researchers and sent them coded computerized messages indicating the new places to search.

"Wake up," his SSA barked. "You're fading out on me, buddy. I need you to be alert."

"Should I start rounding up suspects? Taking them into custody? I could use the local FBI."

"You told me you didn't trust the other feds in town. That's why I took Sheeran off the case."

"Right." He didn't trust anybody. Not the FBI or the air force or Angelica's dad. But he couldn't arrest them all.

"I sure as hell hope this investigation isn't based on some kind of lover's quarrel."

"With Sheeran? Hah! There's nothing between us. There never was."

"That's not how I heard it."

"You heard wrong."

"Come on, Spence, level with me. You're good at your job, but sometimes you get careless, especially when women are involved."

"Not this time," he said. "I've never been so cautious. Angelica turned my computer into an encoded device, which, as you well know, can be hacked, but it's harder. And I'm talking to you on a burner phone that can't be traced."

His years of undercover work had taught him to keep several alternate communications devices. When he ended his call, Spence was irritated. He was juggling as many balls as he could keep in the air and didn't need to be bothered with old gossip and innuendo.

He heard a rap on the hotel suite door. Looking through the peephole, he saw the great, big, redheaded problem glaring back at him. He whipped the door open.

"Not a good time, Sheeran."

"You can call me Raquel." She tried to enter, but he blocked her path. "We're friends, aren't we?"

"I'm busy."

"Too bad."

She jammed a straight arm against his chest and shoved. She dodged to the left, agile as a running back, but she was wearing her high-heeled boots. The only way he'd keep her out would be to tackle her, and that wasn't going to happen.

He stepped aside. "What do you want?"

"An honest update," she said. "There's something big happening, and I'm out of the loop."

"The decision was made at Quantico." Keeping her out was his idea, but he didn't actually issue the orders. "Take it up with them."

"This is my town, where I have my contacts and my snitches. I've got relationships with just about everybody."

"I'll bet you do."

"This isn't right. I should be in charge."

Angelica strolled into the room. After a night of tension and very little sleep, she should have been a wreck, but the color in her cheeks was high and her jaw thrust forward. She looked as formidable as her father, without the bushy eyebrows.

"Technically," she said, "I'm in charge. This isn't a matter of seniority but of expertise. Bottom line, it's a cyber crime. And I'm the expert."

"At least tell me the crime."

"You reported it," Angelica said. "The black hats are knocking on the door, hacking at NORAD and trying to steal our military secrets."

Spence was impressed by the way she danced at the edge of the truth without actually betraying any information. He was more inclined to take physical action, picking up the SSA bodily and hurling her through the door.

Sheeran wasn't going anywhere. With an unwarranted sense of entitlement, she planted her bottom on the sofa. "I'm here to help. I'll do anything."

Angelica tested the offer. "Would you please make a fresh pot of coffee?"

Instead of flaring up, Sheeran went to the landline phone in the suite and called room service. In addition to coffee, she ordered breakfast.

He pulled Angelica into the bathroom and

closed the door. "You've got to get rid of her. She's up to something."

"How do you know?"

"You're going to have to trust me," he said, "the same way I trusted you to fly that tin can through the night skies."

"You also said something about keeping your enemies close. We shouldn't tell Sheeran what we're really investigating, but she might be useful."

"The way a mongoose is useful to a cobra," he muttered.

She patted his cheek, which was clean-shaven again. He expected to be dealing with military personnel today, and they appreciated grooming. Following that line of thinking, he'd put on a button-down shirt with his jeans. A navy blazer would go over his shoulder holster.

Likewise, Angelica wore a fitted black pantsuit with sensible boots and a rose gold chain. She fiddled with the matching, engraved locket that dangled from the chain. "I spoke to Lambert, and he's arranged for us to get into the Cheyenne Mountain Complex this morning."

"We're not taking Sheeran there, are we?"

"Actually, I was thinking of inviting a few others. I'd like to have Fletch with me."

He shouldn't have to remind her that her former mentor was one of their suspects. "Why?"

"He knows more about the old computers than I do."

They were assembling a potentially combustible group, but she might be right about keeping a close watch on the enemy. If Spence was standing over them, none of these people could launch a missile.

THE DRIVE UP the side of Cheyenne Mountain to the North Portal entrance was winding and steep. After yesterday's blue skies, another cold front had moved in. It hadn't yet started snowing, but the wind battered their SUV, promising worse weather to come.

Spence drove the lead vehicle in their little caravan. He'd insisted on riding alone with Angelica so they'd have a chance to talk without being overheard. Holding in all the sensitive information while outsiders hovered wasn't easy. And the outsiders had multiplied.

Following them in another SUV, SSA Sheeran brought along her two coworkers, SA Ramirez and SA Tapper. Bringing up the rear was Dunne, Lambert and Professor Fletcher. It was a motley crew, held together by curiosity and mistrust.

With his hands-free phone, he'd spoken to his supervisor and discovered that not much had been accomplished. No other missiles had been discovered and deactivated. The total stood at four, which made it even more important for Angelica to figure out the computers and stop any attempt to launch.

Spence's supervisor had communicated with Angelica's bosses at Cyber Security, and her supervisor spoke to her. After he complimented her work, he issued an order.

"We have decided, in conjunction with the FBI, to stop investigating at six o'clock MST. At that time, you and Spence will step down."

Not what she wanted to hear. "Should we return to headquarters?"

"I'd like for you to stay on as an observer. The military will be called in and NORAD will go on high alert."

She swallowed hard, choking back her fear. This would be the moment when the fighter jets scrambled and other silos were opened and ready to strike back. "What if we need more time?"

"That's a risk we can't take. We need to be prepared for the assault."

Before he hung up, Angelica thanked him. "I appreciate that you let me contact Professor Fletcher as a consultant. I need his expert advice."

Her supervisor signed off with words of encouragement. Angelica had never heard this tough, taciturn federal agent sound so sincere. Nuclear threats had a way of bringing out the best in people. Or the worst.

She reached across the console and patted Spence's arm. "Did you get the word about pulling the plug on our investigation at six?"

"That only leaves us a few hours to find the people behind this scheme and to end it."

Tension squeezed her lungs. She was breathless. "Do you think we can do it?"

"We can do anything."

She appreciated his bravado. "On a totally different topic, I want to thank you. When the professor insisted that Dunne come along, you agreed."

"He's a loon."

"I don't know why the professor likes him."

"The first time I saw him today, Dunne told me that he was sure Lambert killed Heller. Apparently, Lambert confided to him that he'd left the professor's house to make a quick run to the store."

"Did he suggest a motive?" she asked. "Why would Lambert shoot his friend?"

"Professional jealousy."

"Of what? They both work in midlevel jobs at Peterson AFB." She held up her hand. "Wait! Let me guess, they were doing a computer start-up. It's the sad, well-worn story of Jobs and Wozniak at Apple."

"According to Dunne, they didn't aim that high," he said. "They're inventing the software for a game together."

"And why, according to him, did Lambert feel compelled to take a photo?"

"Dunne didn't have an answer for that one, but he tells the rest of the story convincingly.

When sociopaths lie, they flesh out details, almost believing the lie really happened."

"How dangerous is he?"

"I don't think he'll try anything when he's surrounded by gun-toting air force personnel."

Dunne and Fletcher would be accompanied and supervised every step of the way. It required Level One clearance to enter the Complex. The FBI agents were another story. They could roam almost at will.

Approaching the three-story-tall Portal door, which stood at an elevation of about seven thousand feet, Spence marveled at the sheer size and scope of the engineering feat. He'd studied the blueprints for the impregnable bunker. The hollowed-out chambers covered about five acres. There were fifteen buildings and all were three stories tall. The reservoir, filled by a natural spring, was big enough for a rowboat.

Once inside, there was no immediate access to the outside world. Many of the office buildings had windows that displayed a camera feed of the parking lot or farther up the mountain. The ceilings in the main chamber reached high, and the light from the generators kept it from feeling like they were trapped inside a cave. He doubted his minor claustrophobia would bother him.

After they parked, their group clustered while air force guides dressed in camo and berets gave them the basic rules. *Don't touch anything. Don't go wandering off by yourself.*

They also confiscated all weapons and cell phones. Though he hated giving up his own guns, Spence was glad when SSA Sheeran and her two buddies were disarmed. Though he had nothing specific that pointed to their guilt, he didn't trust those three.

They were driven down the main tunnel to the entrance through the twenty-five-ton North blast door. Made of solid steel, the thick door stood open.

"The last time it was closed," the professor said, "was September 11. Our country never needed to use Cheyenne Mountain as a wartime bunker, but that's really what it is."

While Spence inspected the remarkable black door, Angelica asked her former mentor, "When was the first time you visited the Complex?"

"Dear me, it was so long ago. I don't remember the date, but Nixon was President. I was a student at University of Denver, and a bunch of us had a chance to take the tour. The Complex was remarkable. It influenced my decision to stick with computer technology."

On the other side of the blast door was a second protective door, similar to the first. As they proceeded down the corridor leading to the main chamber, Fletch continued to lecture. The man was a teacher, after all. He had a lot to say about the engineering and the excavation. When they came to the buildings, he got down on one knee to examine the hundreds of heavy-duty springs that made up the building's support system.

"These structures can't have basements," he said, "not without pile-driving through bedrock. And so, they used these springs, which serve the purpose of balancing the building in case of an earthquake or a slight shift."

Lambert had sidled up beside Spence. Quietly, he asked, "May I have a word?"

"Make it quick. Angelica might need your help in the computer area."

When they separated from the others, one of the guards stayed behind with them. Spence was glad to see the high level of vigilance.

"You've been talking to Dunne," Lambert said.

"Yes."

Lambert pushed his thick glasses up on his nose. "He's a liar, and he told me to lie about the alibi."

"After you left Heller's apartment, how long were you at the professor's house?"

"The whole time," he said, "But I wasn't with the other two. I was working on software for a gaming system."

"A project you shared with Heller."

"That's right." He stuck a plump finger under his glasses to wipe away a tear. "I don't think I can get it done without him. I'll try, but it was both of us. Sexy Lexy and Big Bo."

The racy characterization of these nerds amused Spence. He bit his lip to keep from smiling. "You were good friends."

"The best."

Dunne peeled off from the main group and charged toward them. Walking and talking at the same time, he said, "Don't listen to this pudgy weasel. He's jealous of me."

"Am not." Lambert stamped his sneaker on the floor. "You're a loser who works at a coffee shop. I'm a computer engineer."

Dunne waved to the professor. "Fletcher, did you hear what he said to me?"

The professor made a clumsy pivot and came back toward them, walking carefully. "Stop fighting, boys."

Angelica accompanied the older man, who clung to her arm as he shuffled along. Spence watched these separate, distinct persons as they arranged themselves in a circle. Dunne, the sociopath, waved his arms and made wild pronouncements about how Lambert was jealous and plotting. Lambert puffed out his chest and objected, although he was clearly intimidated by Dunne. The professor stroked his beard and mumbled in an attempt to make peace. Angelica didn't fit with the others. Though operating under a literal life-and-death situation, she kept her shoulders straight and her mouth shut.

Dunne blasted a final accusation at Lambert. "You think you're real clever with your new game, but the professor thinks it's boring and just like every other game."

"Is that true?" Lambert looked toward Fletch with pleading eyes. "You think I'm boring."

"He's not going to admit it because he's too polite, but I know the truth." Dunne sneered and said, "The old man doesn't like it."

As soon as he spoke, Angelica gasped loudly. When Spence turned and looked at her, he saw recognition in her eyes. She'd told him about hearing the very words that Dunne had spoken.

"It was you." She pointed at Dunne. "You were one of the people who abducted me."

Chapter Twenty-One

Those words about the old man were branded on Angelica's memory. Not even drugs and amnesia managed to erase them. Her first thought was that they were talking about her father, that somehow, he was involved in this treasonous plot. But Dunne had inadvertently named Professor Fletch as the old man who wanted to protect her. The facts didn't make sense. She couldn't believe he would perform such a traitorous act. Could he be the "old man," and still be innocent of the larger crimes?

Spence clamped his huge hand around Dunne's arm like an iron manacle. "You heard what she said. You were part of the group that kidnapped her."

Showing absolutely no remorse, he said, "Maybe I was."

Rather than locking Dunne up and throwing away the key, she watched as Spence tried not to be intimidating. He'd told her that the best way to manage a guy like Dunne was to sit back and let him talk. "Tell me about it."

"You should be thanking me." Dunne pointed at her. "I'm the one that told them not to hurt you. I protected you."

That was a screwy way of looking at kidnapping and dosing her with drugs, but she didn't question his logic. There was something bigger at stake. He had information they needed. If he gave them names, they might be able to arrest the leaders and end the threat.

"I wasn't mistreated." She forced a smile. "And I thank you for the role you played in keeping me unharmed."

"It was all me. The other guys wanted to throw you off the edge of a mountain and see how high you'd bounce…except for the guy with the amnesia drugs. Oh, yeah, that was smart, really smart. We could let you go, and you couldn't rat us out."

"Why did you want to protect me?"

"Don't flatter yourself, babe. I don't have a crush on you." He scoffed at Lambert. "I'm not like him or this old man."

Fletch took Dunne's free hand and held it against his heart. His eyes were terribly sad. "I could have done more for you, Howie Dunne. You're not a bad man, I know you aren't."

"You're the only person who thinks that," he said. "That's why I couldn't let them kill her. If Angelica was hurt, I knew it would make you sad."

Fletch nodded. "You know me well."

"You're like a father, better than my father."

She would have been touched by this deep

friendship if Dunne hadn't been so crazy. His emotions were askew, and his only truth was an admiration for Fletch.

Spence turned Dunne toward him. "Heller was there with you."

"Heller got me into this mess," Dunne said. "He was flashing around all this cash money, always hundreds. It started with easy stuff, dropping off a car or picking up a package. And I got paid a whole lot more than I ever made as a barista."

"What was the price for keeping an eye on Angelica?"

"A cool thousand."

The professor bowed his head. "If you wanted money, all you had to do was ask me."

"I like paying my own way."

She found his rationale totally unbelievable. He was equating his criminal endeavors with an honest day's work. "Did you have any idea what you were doing? Or the risk to other people? Did Heller bother to explain that he and his buddies wanted to nuke an entire city?"

"I found out," he said, "after the fact. They were talking about ICBMs and missile silos."

"And you knew it was wrong," Spence said.

"Before that, right and wrong didn't mean very much."

"You're reading my mind." Dunne gave a short, mirthless laugh. "I went to Heller's house to tell him that I quit. No more of these jobs for me."

"And he told you that you couldn't leave," Spence said.

"So I shot him."

If she gave him the benefit of the doubt, his twisted morality made sense. He had committed murder, thinking he would stop a greater crime. More likely, he killed Heller because their partnership had become inconvenient.

"Were there others?" Spence asked. "Is there anyone else you can name?"

He shook his head. "Are they going to cut off my bun in prison?"

He'd be lucky if that was the only thing that got cut off, but she didn't say anything else.

Spence spoke to their guides for a moment. Then he returned to the group, still holding on to Dunne's arm. "I know Angelica's anxious to get started. Lambert and the professor will accompany her, and I'll catch up later."

"We'll go with Spence," SSA Sheeran said. "He might need our help interrogating this killer."

Angelica didn't gloat over Sheeran's failure as an interrogator. She'd had the first chance to question Dunne when she picked him up at the hotel that first night. Also, she'd spent significant time with him over the last few days. Was she keeping something a secret? What did she think she could do to get him talking?

She walked a few paces, flanked by Lambert and the professor. The old man's step slowed to a crawl, and she sent one of their escorts to find a wheelchair for him. They sat on a bench outside one of the buildings.

"It feels like we're waiting for a bus," she said as she took the professor's hand. "But this Complex is a bit small for mass transit."

Lambert piped up, "I've seen a couple of those little electric cars. Those could be taxis."

"Professor," she said, "I'm sorry about Dunne."

"The boy is sick, very sick. I thought I could save him and get him on the right track, but my help just wasn't enough." Inside his beard, he smiled sadly. "I try to heal all the young people I mentor."

"Not me," she said.

"Not you," Lambert echoed. "You're perfect."

But she hadn't been this confident when the professor took her under his wing. In addition to learning computers, they'd spent hours talking. Back in those days, she'd been so afraid of failing her father that she was almost paralyzed by that fear. Fletch helped her separate from him, and then she had learned to leave her mentor behind, too.

"You've changed," the professor said. "But you're still attracted to strong men, like Spence."

"Is he good for me?"

"You have to decide for yourself."

When he was seated in the wheelchair, they proceeded to the storage area for input data and computers. A regular business would have thrown all this outdated stuff away, but Cheyenne Mountain Complex was an air force installation, and the military never threw away anything.

"What are we looking for?" Lambert asked.

"Software that can be used to activate missiles from the late fifties or early sixties, and we need to find a computer that can process that software."

"A history project," he said brightly.

Fletcher gave them an idea of earmarks to

look for while he searched for a machine that was still in working condition. The whole process gave her a greater appreciation for the early days of computers. Their functions might not have been as complex as current machines, but the innovation was stunning.

For over an hour, she and Lambert dug through a mountain of data. When they found promising software, they placed it on a table in front of Fletch. He did further study on several, but none got the thumbs-up.

She was glad to be busy. The activity kept her mind off the ticktock counting down to six o'clock, when the military would be put on high alert and the missile launch would be almost inevitable.

She placed a spreadsheet with dot matrix printing in front of the professor. "This looks like it has something to do with a launch. And it's dated 1959."

He tilted his head to see through his bifocals

and slowly nodded. "You might have something significant here."

She sat beside him at the worktable as he plugged codes into the old computer console Lambert had uncovered. After only a few minutes, the printout came rolling out in the form of ticker tape.

"We're on the right track," the professor said.

She sent one of the guards to find Spence and bring him back here. He needed to know about the progress they'd made and to pass that information on to his boss. If other silos had been uncovered, they might be able to deactivate the launch from here. In the meantime, she and Lambert and the Professor continued to shift and adjust and input and print.

The guard returned and pulled her aside. "I can't find him."

"What about Sheeran and the other FBI agents?"

"Also missing."

The time was half past two. There was probably a reasonable explanation for Spence disappearing with Dunne, but she couldn't think of anything right now. She returned to the worktable, where the professor and Lambert were still trying to figure out what they had.

"Stay here," she said firmly. "Don't let anyone in unless they're with me."

She repeated those instructions to the guards. Then she was out of the computer storage building. Spence and the others were supposed to be in the communications command center, another three-story building with offices and video rooms. Running through the Complex without protection was foolish; she'd already been abducted once and didn't want it to happen again. At random, she approached two armed military police, who were dressed in green camouflage and held rifles. "Excuse me," she said. "I need your help."

The young men exchanged a glance. "Sorry,

ma'am, we have an assignment and can't leave our post."

"My father is General Thorne." There were times when it was essential to pull rank. "Make the necessary call, get permission to leave your post and come with me."

After they spoke into a walkie-talkie for a moment, they faced her and saluted. "At your service, Special Agent Thorne."

"I'm looking for some FBI agents." She gave a description of the group. "They were supposed to be in this building, but I think I know a better way to search than running from place to place. Have you got security cameras?"

They escorted her to the area where several security screens covered the wall. Before she could even describe Spence and the others, the supervisor, a civilian, pulled up photos from the IDs they had handed over at the gate.

"Handy," she said. There wasn't an expectation of privacy in a supersecure location like this one. "Can you track these four?"

"Over what time period?"

"The past hour," she said.

She watched the screen that showed the entrance to the communications building. They had entered together. There were a few images of them inside the building, but the interior surveillance wasn't as pervasive as the exterior.

"Over here." The supervisor pointed to a screen that showed water lapping against the walls of a cavern. "That's our reservoir. Nobody is supposed to be there without permission."

But there was a man, running. He wore a crazy Hawaiian shirt. It had to be Dunne. "When was this taken?"

"It's happening right now."

She turned to the air force guys she'd recruited at random. "Take me there."

"You might want to wait," the supervisor said.

Angelica turned her attention to the drama

being played out on the surveillance screen. Dunne had jumped into a rowboat that was attached to a very short dock. He yanked the mooring loose, but before he could shove off, he froze.

Though there was no sound on the surveillance screen, she saw Dunne's mouth moving and imagined him shouting at someone who was unseen in this camera view. Dunne threw both hands over his head.

Before he could climb from the boat, he was shot in the chest. He crumpled onto the deck.

Chapter Twenty-Two

Spence had seen trouble coming, but he was unable to stop it. He rolled onto his side, propped himself up on his right elbow and pried open his eyelids. Blood soaked the shoulder of his sport jacket. He painfully twisted around, trying to apply pressure. If the knife had been a few inches lower, he would have had a punctured lung.

Where was he? The wall behind him was granite. He stared at the white, tightly coiled, heavy-duty springs that supported the weight of the building. How did he get here?

A wave of nausea swept over him. He closed

his eyes and tried to remember what had happened.

He'd just finished his interview with Dunne when Sheeran joined him in the office he'd been using at the communication center. Both he and Dunne had gone silent when she entered. A sense of danger had pervaded the room. With the high heels on her boots clunking on the tile floor, she'd circled the desk.

Her attack had been fast and deadly. She yanked Dunne from his chair and held him in front of her with a sharp, thin blade aimed at his carotid artery.

"Do what I say, Spence. Or he dies."

"How did you get the knife past the metal detector?"

"It's high-grade plastic, sharp enough to slice through metal. I always carry an extra weapon in my boot."

Her instructions to him had been simple. She wanted him to use his handcuffs and fasten himself to the desk, stay in this office and let her get away.

"I don't have cuffs with me," he said. "What did you do with the other two agents?"

"They work for me." Her cool grin was pure evil. "Agent Tapper, my computer expert, will launch the strike against Dallas. Ramirez has international contacts."

"Ramirez," Dunne piped up. "I thought I recognized him. Was he running the kidnapping?"

"And not doing a very good job at it," she said. "He got nervous about killing Angelica, didn't want to be responsible for the murder of a federal agent."

Yet, he didn't seem to mind blowing up an entire city?

Spence hoped and prayed that the expert researchers had managed to find and deactivate the rest of the silos. There wasn't much time left, and he was pretty sure he wouldn't be able to stop this crazy witch. She was revealing details that she shouldn't tell, which meant that whether or not he had cuffs, she had to kill him.

"Why are you doing this?" he asked.

"It's my legacy. The millions I get from selling these warheads are my inheritance from my loving father, who never quite got his act together. Did I mention that he worked right here at Cheyenne Mountain Complex?"

"You said he served under General Thorne."

"And also right here. Last year, he died and told me what he'd done."

"Fifty years ago, your father took seven missile silos off-line," Spence said.

"I'm impressed," she said. "You and your little sweetie figured that out. What else do you know?"

"Here's what I don't understand," he said. "Why did you report the hack? Why call attention to it?"

"To cover my behind," she said. "Heller showed me the paperwork, and I soft-pedalled it. Everybody hacks everybody else, and nobody much cares. I mean, look at the FBI response to my report that there's evidence of hacking at NORAD. After a few, they send two agents pretending to be undercover. Pathetic."

Dunne wriggled in her arms, and she drew her blade across his cheek. Blood ran down his face. "If it weren't for this moron and his friend Heller stirring up trouble, I would have gotten away with this."

"Angelica found your advertising on the dark web."

"So I've heard." She sneered. "That was one of the secrets she blabbed when she was kidnapped and drugged. When it comes to computers, she's smart. Not so much when it comes to men. You're still commitment-phobic. Right, Spence?"

"There was never anything between you and me," he said.

"You wanted me." Her eyes flashed with

anger. "I was smart enough to get out before it got too serious."

He stood and kicked back the desk chair behind him. "Do you really think you can blow up Dallas and walk away?"

"Sit down," she said.

He'd figured out his attack. If she was good with a knife, and he suspected she was, she could slice Dunne's carotid and still have time to throw the blade at him. He had to strike first, and there was a paperweight on the desk—a pretty glass ball with swirls inside. He'd throw the weight as a distraction, and then go after her.

He eased around the edge of the desk. Gradually, he was coming into range. "Have you gotten any bidders?"

"They're all waiting to see the first strike."

He considered for a moment. Then he played his last card. "You might want to reconsider."

"Why?"

"We've been tracking down your off-line silos and having them deactivated. Your legacy is already spent."

"You couldn't have done them all."

"We found one by Sterling and another near Grand Junction."

She seemed to be distracted. This was his moment. He flung the paperweight and scored a direct hit against her forehead. It wasn't hard enough to knock her out, but she loosened her grip on Dunne and lowered the knife. He jumped at her and knocked her knife hand out of the way. Dunne scrambled to his feet and rushed through the exit from the office.

Sheeran yelled to her cohorts in the hallway. "Stop him."

She hadn't dropped the knife. Flailing wildly, she lashed out and hit him below the left shoulder. The sharpened plastic plunged through flesh and sinew, but his arm still functioned.

He found the paperweight on the floor and

used it again. This time, he aimed at her knife hand. With a yelp, she dropped her weapon and dashed out the door, which she locked behind her.

His shoulder should have hurt like hellfire. He was losing a lot of blood. But his adrenaline level was so high that he hardly felt the pain. He kicked at the door, which was, like everything else in the Complex, solid. Thinking there might be a key in the desk drawer, he yanked open the drawers.

No key, but he saw a little .21 caliber handgun in the upper right drawer. It would have been useful to have that earlier. He armed himself. The blood pouring from his wound made the floor slippery and he stumbled. His head whacked against the corner of the desk. His world went dark.

ANGELICA PACED IN the rear of the computer room while Professor Fletcher and Lambert worked to locate the silos and take the missiles off-line. Their work—combined with that of the other FBI researchers—had resulted in five sites being deactivated. Only two were left, barely enough to make the sale profitable, especially if one missile was used for the strike.

It made sense for the hacker to back down and cancel the auction. There was no reason to attack Dallas. Nothing important would be gained or lost. If they could contact the person in charge, they might be able to negotiate.

"I'm so close," Fletch said. "If I had the valid code, I could access the launch sequence and shut down the entire operation."

"What kind of code is it?" she asked. "Numbers? Letters? A binary sequence?"

"Not that complicated," he said. "Six or seven letters or numbers."

She tried to recall all the information she'd scanned and studied, hoping a password would become apparent. "Try Y75110 or Office1116. There was another one. Oh, C4ICBM."

Throwing out those codes indicated a deep level of desperation. She was beginning to lose hope, and she was scared. Spence had disappeared along with the other FBI agents, and an unidentified person had shot Dunne. Spence might be next. Or the killer might be coming for her and Fletch and Bo.

If Spence wasn't injured, she was sure he'd come for her. He'd sworn to protect her. She clenched her jaw. He should have been the one wearing the implanted GPS chip so she could always find him.

Two guards dressed in camo entered the room. "We have information, Agent Thorne."

Her heart plummeted. "Did you find Spence?"

"Not yet. We're still searching."

She pulled them aside, hoping to shield the professor and Lambert. "Tell me."

"Howard Dunne died on the way to the hospital."

Though she hadn't liked Dunne, a stab of remorse hit her in the gut. "Did he have last words?"

The guard nodded. "For the Professor."

From outside the building, she heard an alarm squawking and blaring so loudly that she automatically covered her ears with her hands. A voice on the public-address system told them that this "was not a drill." There were in the midst of a "Level Three threat."

She looked to the guards. "Level Three? What does that mean?"

"Prepare for nuclear attack."

They were too late. The strike was already underway.

"What should we do? Is there a safe room?"

"Ma'am, this entire mountain is a safety bunker."

Professor Fletch joined them. He was beaming as he shouted over the alarm. "I've got it. One of the codes you gave me busted through. C4ICBM is the answer."

"Can you shut down the launch?"

"I think so." He bobbed his head. "You don't look happy. What's gone wrong?"

There was no good way to deliver this news. "I hate to tell you this. Dunne was shot in the stomach. On the way to the hospital, he died."

The guard in camouflage spoke up. "His last words were for the medics to tell Fletch that he loved him."

The old man sank into the chair where he'd been working frantically, and he lowered his head. When she kissed his cheek, she tasted his salty tears.

"I'm sorry," she whispered.

"Go," he said.

"What?"

"I've heard your sigh and seen you pacing. You're worried about Spence. Lambert and

I will disable the launch while you go find your man."

She didn't need to be told twice. Grabbing one of the armed guards, she dashed from the building.

SPENCE WOKE TO the sound of an alarm blasting and a voice on the PA system telling them about the threat. Special Agent Jay Ramirez knelt beside him, tugging at his arm.

"Wake up," Ramirez said. "Come on, man, we've got to get out of here."

"Stop pushing me," Spence growled. "We can't leave. Level Three means that Cheyenne Mountain is closed down with the blast doors shut tight. Nobody gets out."

When he tried to stand, the pounding in the back of his skull was nearly as painful as the shoulder wound. Ramirez handed him a bottle of water.

"Drink it all," he said. "You're probably de-hydrated."

"Did you drug me?"

"Hell, yes. Every time I tried to help, you'd take a swing at me. I gave you a sedative, and you're welcome."

"How did we get to this spot?"

"Your fault," he said. "Sheeran locked you in, and it took me a while to get the door open. When I did, you were gone. You'd climbed out of the second floor window. I figured it was a clever way to avoid all the cameras, and I followed."

"Why are you helping me?"

"When I found out what Sheeran was really doing, I had to stop her. I'm not officially undercover, but I kind of am."

"I'll vouch for you."

"I was hoping you'd say that." He urged Spence forward. "We should go to Command Central where they have the big screens. We can watch the fireworks. And you can get somebody to patch up that shoulder."

"What fireworks?"

"You don't think these technology geniuses are going to let Sheeran nuke Dallas, do you? There's got to be a counter strike. When those missiles start flying, I want to watch."

"We have to stop her," Spence said. "Where is she?"

"I'm not sure, but she's going to need an old-fashioned computer system for Tapper to make the launch. Where would she find equipment like that?"

"The computer storage area." He glugged the rest of the water. Adrenaline pulsed through his veins. "Angelica is in that building."

When he stumbled around the corner of the three-story building, he saw empty streets as the alarm continued to split the air. Everyone had a specific job in case of a threat. He needed to be with her. Never should have left her alone.

Why didn't he learn after the first abduction? He had to protect her. She was his world, the only woman he ever truly loved.

With Ramirez jogging at his side, Spence headed toward the computer storage building. He held his left arm stiffly, trying to keep from jostling the wound. With his right hand, he felt the .21 caliber handgun that he'd taken from the desk drawer. He hoped he wouldn't have to use it. The military could take care of Sheeran and Tapper.

The door to the computer building flew open, and Angelica came out. She dashed toward him with her arms wide-open, but she didn't grab him when she got close.

"You're hurt."

He truly didn't feel it. "We've got to hide."

"We can't leave the professor in there un-guarded."

"Get him." They could all go at the same time.

"Not yet," she said. "He's almost done."

He allowed her to drag him into the computer room on the first floor. A couple of guards in green camo helped him to a chair in the back of the room. He didn't ask to be fussed over but didn't object when they dressed his wound.

The alarm went silent, finally. He shook his head, trying to clear it. Again, it felt like he went unconscious. When he looked up, there was his sweet angel sitting beside him.

The door behind her opened, and Sheeran marched in. She had her knife in one hand and a gun in the other. "If anybody moves, I start shooting."

One of the guards reached for his weapon and she fired a bullet into his Kevlar vest, knocking him backward.

Her demands were ferocious. "Whatever the hell you're doing in here to shut down my computer, stop it. Now."

"You're too late," Angelica said. "It's over."

Spence could see Sheeran's intention as she

lifted her gun. He was quicker. With a flip of his wrist, he drew his weapon and fired twice. He hit her in the arm and in the leg. The .21 wasn't a powerful weapon, but it was enough to stop her.

As soon as she went down, the guards took her into custody. Then, they went upstairs to pick up Special Agent Tapper.

Ramirez was the only man left standing. And he had a hell of a lot of explaining to do.

With the threat ended, Angelica directed Spence down a hallway to a small, quiet office. She made him sit.

"We did it," she said.

"Your first field assignment was a success."

She filled him in on how she and Fletch had broken the codes. He told her about Sheeran and her father's strange legacy.

"Dunne was murdered," she said.

"That poor fool," Spence said with a shake of his head. "He actually was trying to turn his life around. The reason he took the photo of Heller was so he could show it to the professor and have him figure out the danger."

"Dunne didn't want a strike on Dallas?"

"He said he wasn't a monster. And he knew that killing all those people would be wrong. I misjudged him."

They sat quietly for a moment, contemplating what had happened and what might have been.

"I messed a lot of things up on this assignment," he said. "Can I still get a do-over?"

"That depends on what you want to do."

"The first time I told you I loved you, it wasn't very romantic. So I wanted to do this right."

Gently, she wrapped her arms around him. "I love you back."

"You're getting blood all over your clothes," he said.

"I don't care." She kissed his forehead, then his chin. "Tell me again."

"I'll go one better." He took a small velvet

box from his pocket and opened the lid. "Marry me, Angelica."

Without hesitation, she accepted.

"Is your dad going to be okay with this?"

"It's not his decision."

"And do you trust me?"

She stared at the diamond glittering on her finger. "Without trust, there can't be love."

He couldn't agree more.

* * * * *